EAST R...

INFORMATION SERVICE

WITHDRAWN FROM STOCK

WULF, Linda Press
The night of the burning

POCKLINGTON

D0489463

Night

## of the

# Burning

# The
# Night
## of the
# Burning

### LINDA PRESS WULF

**BLOOMSBURY**

East Riding of Yorkshire
Library and Information
Services

901 201442 5

Askews

£5.99

Pac          Junior Fic

First published in Great Britain in 2007 by Bloomsbury Publishing Plc
36 Soho Square, London, W1D 3QY

This paperback edition first published in 2008

First published in the USA by Farrar, Straus and Giroux in 2006

Copyright © 2006 Linda Press Wulf
The moral right of the author has been asserted

All rights reserved
No part of this publication may be reproduced or
transmitted by any means, electronic, mechanical, photocopying
or otherwise, without the prior permission of the publisher

A CIP catalogue record of this book is available from the British Library

ISBN 978 0 7475 9134 4

All papers used by Bloomsbury Publishing are natural, recyclable products
made from wood grown in well-managed forests. The manufacturing processes
conform to the environmental regulations of the country of origin.

Printed in Great Britain by Clays Ltd, St Ives Plc

1 3 5 7 9 10 8 6 4 2

www.bloomsbury.com

*For my husband's mother, the Devorah Lehrman of this story,*
*whom I never met*
*For my own mother, who shared my love of old-fashioned books*
*for children*
*For my father, who taught me about crafting words*
*For my siblings, whose support and critical direction were*
*essential to this story*
*For my Aunty Rhoda in the book-lined house on Avenue*
*Normandie*
*For my husband and sons, who make my life good*

# Contents

# The Orphanage in Pinsk, Poland

## 1921

I didn't giggle. Since the Night of the Burning, I hadn't laughed. I knew I would never laugh again. The other children giggled behind their hands at the funny hat on the man who was visiting our orphanage. It was a firm brown felt hat that sailed on the top of his head like a boat, very different from the soft caps most men crammed down over their ears in our snowy Polish winters.

I stared at the strange man as he sat with the orphanage director, Alexander Bobrow, at the head of the old table where we ate our breakfast. He looked friendly and clean and soft. He reminded me a little of Papa. Papa's face had been soft before he became so thin.

Maybe the strange man felt me staring at him through his skin, the way you feel the sun through your closed eyelids in the early morning, because suddenly he glanced up and smiled right at me.

Quickly I looked down and pretended to be absorbed in spooning up my lumpy porridge. I knew that when the bowl was empty, I would still not feel satisfied; there was never enough to fill my belly all the way to the top.

Sitting right next to me, Nechama was one of the children who giggled. Just like those other silly little girls. How dare she giggle; how dare she even smile? At nine years old, she was just a baby, so immature compared with me. I was twelve. I hated that she acted as if our lives had begun when the hay cart brought us here to the orphanage in Pinsk, less than a year before. There she sat, chattering brightly to two girls she called her "best friends." I moved my chair firmly and loudly closer to hers. She was behaving as if she were actually happy. But whenever I talked about Mama and Papa, she squirmed away. I wanted so badly to talk about Mama and Papa. And I couldn't talk to anyone else.

Nechama had finished her breakfast. She was touching her own hair admiringly and she lifted her clear eyes to me, not even noticing that I was angry.

"The big girls said that man will choose me. They said my curls are so pretty he'll be sure to want me," she said, twirling the soft wisps around her fingers.

"Which man? Choose you for what?"

"That man from Africa," Nechama said, pointing at the stranger. "He's taking children to Africa!" Then she caught sight of Malke leaving the room, jumped from her stool at the table, and ran off after her friend.

Africa. I turned the word over slowly in my mouth. It was open and hot, a word that hung in the air—Africah-ah. Not like the quick, lip-pursed word Europe. What was Nechama running on about? Some wild gossip made up by her new friends? Not a serious thought in their heads; just play and laugh, play and laugh.

I cleared both of our bowls from the table and wandered to the empty dormitory to sit on my straw mattress. Pulling my thick braid across my cheek, I chewed on the bristly end. There was a round black stove in the corner of the room, but the metal was icy cold. The grownups said we were short of coal. I wrapped my coat tightly around my chest and tried to pull the sleeves down farther, but the coat was meant for someone smaller. The skin on my fingers was cracked and red.

Squeezing one hand into my pocket for warmth, I felt the stiff paper of a photograph. Papa had given it to me before he died, and I always kept it in my pocket. After the Night of the Burning, when Nechama and I left our village on the hay cart to Pinsk, it was all I had with me. I didn't even need to glance at it to see it clearly. In the photo our whole family was together, as in a dream—Papa and Mama side by side, Nechama a tiny baby in Mama's arms, me on Papa's knee. We were all smiling.

I must have drifted into sleep on my mattress. I was dreaming about Mama's latkes. Usually Mama would cook the potato pancakes on the iron sheet on top of the stove, but at Chanukah she fried them in precious, expensive oil.

"Ah, Mama," Papa would sigh with satisfaction. "The pancakes are like angels singing."

"More, Mama, more, Mama, more!" I would chant, and of course Nechama copied me.

Someone was shaking my shoulder gently. I groaned, trying to hold on to my dream. I was so happy being in my old life again. But the shaking continued and I opened my eyes a little. Mr. Bobrow's face was looking down at me and his free hand was pushing his round spectacles back as they slipped down his nose. It was the director himself shaking my shoulder. I sat up immediately, wide awake. Where was the danger? Where was Nechama?

"Come, sad one," Mr. Bobrow said. "Mr. Isaac Ochberg wants to meet you. He noticed your big eyes looking at him at breakfast, and he wants to see if he can put a smile on that face. He's waiting for you."

"Nechama?" I whispered.

"Nechama's fine; she's playing with her friends," Mr. Bobrow said reassuringly. He patted my shoulder again with that concerned look on his face. "It's all right, Devorah. You don't have to be so scared all the time."

I looked away so he wouldn't see how angry that made me. Could he give his promise on the holy Torah that I didn't have to be frightened? What if I stopped being on the watch for danger, and something happened again?

I climbed off the mattress silently, pulled down my tight coat, and tied back my hair with shaking hands. Trailing behind Mr. Bobrow's long legs, I followed him to the dining room. My anger had leaked away; now I was just plain scared. He pointed at the door, which was slightly ajar. He was sending me all alone into a room where a stranger waited.

"Come in with me," I managed to whisper.

"You'll be fine," he replied. "You're a lucky girl." And then he walked off down the hallway. Me, lucky?

I tiptoed to the door and peered through the opening. The man called Isaac Ochberg sat reading a stack of papers. He had no whiskers on his round clean face; his ears stood out from his wavy reddish hair. Except that he wears that hat and has no beard, he looks like people from home, I thought. But my right eyelid was twitching from nervousness. Should I go in? Should I run away and find Ne-chama? Should I knock? Or just wait?

Suddenly Isaac Ochberg looked up and smiled at me the way he had at breakfast. There were big smile creases around his mouth. I slipped inside.

"Come here, little one, little"—he consulted the top paper in his pile and continued—"Devorah Lehrman. And your younger sister is Nechama, am I right?"

I nodded.

The man patted the bench next to him, and I sat down warily. "I'll explain why I am here," he began. "I've come a long way, from a country called South Africa, down at the tip of Africa. There are Jewish people there, and they're worried about all the children in Europe who have no fathers and mothers because of the Great War. And that craziness they call the Russian Revolution."

I knew about the Great War and the Russian Revolution, but they meant nothing to me. I only thought about the morning when we tucked Papa's blankets in to try to keep him warm, when he was already dead. And I thought about Mama before she died, calling for more water, more water, as the typhoid burned her from inside. I thought about the flames galloping through our village, the synagogue glowing red against the night.

I shook my head to get rid of those thoughts. I needed to concentrate on the strange things Mr. Ochberg was saying. "So they sent me to find two hundred children and bring them back to South Africa. It's a beautiful country and a safe place for Jews. I'll take you and your little sister. But only if you really want to go with me."

I frowned at him in amazement. What did he mean?

"Do you want to come with me, Devorah—you and Nechama?"

I heard a huge gasp coming from my chest. Move to another country? That place called Africa? With a man Nechama and I didn't know? My lips were quivering and my whole body had begun to shake.

The man looked at me closely. "Life will be better there, Devorah. You will have food and a warm, clean place to live. And you will go to school. You will even have toys and dolls. Have you ever seen a doll before, a really beautiful doll?"

A really beautiful doll. I could see in my mind, feel in my hands, not one but two stuffed dolls in embroidered dresses, one for me and the other for Nechama. Papa had bought them one year when the potato harvest was good and the peasants had plenty of money to buy his wares. Never before had we seen such elegant creatures. We wrapped them in clean rags and played with them only inside, only after washing our hands. I felt a burning behind my eyes. I hadn't cried for months; I knew if I cried, I would split into pieces. I pressed my fingers hard against my eyelids.

The man moved closer and put his arm around me. "Mamaleh," he murmured, "I know it has been terrible, mamaleh."

Another raw gasp shot out of me. With one scoop, the man cradled me against him as if I were a small child, as if I were Nechama. I felt a deep hum in his chest as he began to sing,

"Inter yideles vigele
Shtayt a klur-vas tsigele . . .

Under the baby's cradle,
stands a little white goat . . ."

I knew that lullaby. Papa and Mama had sung it to us many times. "It hurts," I moaned. "Hurts." The pain would tear me apart; I could not bear to let the pain out.

The man tightened his arms around me and I found myself gripping his wool sleeve, burrowing my face into its warmth. Sobs scraped my throat, rough, ragged sobs. The wool grew wet as I cried for my heart that was broken and my family that was broken and my home that was broken and would never be whole again.

My body was jerking, but the man held me strongly and went on singing,

> ". . . Rozhinkes mit mandlen;
> Shluf zhe, yidele, shluf.
>
> Raisins and almonds;
> Sleep, my little one, sleep."

# A Village Called Domachevo
## 1915–16

The dolls were not the first presents that Papa had bought for us, but they were by far the best. He took them slowly out of his pockets one night when I was almost six and Nechama almost three. We were sitting close to the glowing stove and feeling happy to have our papa home again after one of his longer trips.

"Here is a very fine lady," he announced dramatically, "who would like to meet my Devorahleh." He waved a doll above my face as I gaped. Then Nechama yelped when Papa pulled out a companion doll.

"May I introduce Nechama, too, O beautiful ladies?" he asked the dolls seriously.

We shrieked and threw our arms around the warm hill that was Papa's belly. Then we reached for his presents.

"Look, Mama, see how tiny the embroidery stitches are on their aprons," I said, running my fingers over the miniature red and green flowers.

"They have real white stockings," Nechama said, "and see the nice fat legs."

"They're not Jewish girls," I pointed out. "See, their eyes are blue buttons and their hair is yellow wool, just like the Christian villagers' on the other side of the pond."

"So, you're telling me that the peasant girls in Domachevo have blue buttons for eyes?" Papa asked with a straight face.

"Oh, Papa, you know I mean the colors!" I giggled. Papa and I had the same dark wavy hair, while Nechama had Mama's light brown curls. And Mama's prettiness, too, I had to admit to myself. I knew Mama loved Nechama best sometimes, and I knew why: Nechama was so pretty and cuddly and small. So easy to love.

Mama smiled and offered Papa some lumps of sugar to hold in his mouth while he drank his tea with loud, comfortable slurps.

"How were things in Brest?" Mama asked. Brest Litovsk was a big town a full day's journey from Domachevo. Papa went there by horse and cart to buy the goods he sold to peasants and Jews in nearby villages.

"A good trip, thank God," Papa answered. "I bought a few tools and knives and some large leather skins. Linen was expensive, but I recognized an old, yellowed roll, which had not been sold since my last trip, and I purchased it for a low price. The peasant women are not particular about the color of their cloth as long as I have bright ribbons, and those I bought aplenty. Pennywhistles for the children. And the foodstuffs."

"May I help you divide the sugar and cinnamon?" I burst in, and Nechama chorused, "Me too!"

"Not only the sweet stuff," Mama chided. "You will help tomorrow night with the salt scoops and the pepper in paper cones, also."

Mama had never been to Brest, nor had many of the Jews in our village, and we were proud of our well-traveled papa. When he returned, his coat smelled different, with scents I didn't recognize. At least one of the knobby-shaped packages swaddled in cloth that he brought home would contain a little surprise for Nechama and me. Although we were as poor as our neighbors, we felt we were the luckiest among our playmates because we had several toys each.

When we wanted to play with our precious dolls, we did not take them outside to the muddy yard, where the neighbor's ducks left squishy green droppings and pecked at the wilted leaves of Mama's potatoes. No, we took off our rough clogs and left them on the clean-swept earthen floor. Then we climbed up the little wooden step and onto Mama and Papa's high bed. We pulled the heavy white cover over our shoulders, feeling the goose feathers shifting with soft whooshes. The cover made a dark cave where we could play house.

I lifted my doll's skirt to see how the legs attached to the torso. Nechama giggled, but then she did the same thing.

"You don't have to copy me all the time," I said irritably. Nechama just giggled again. And actually I didn't really want her to stop copying.

"Easter is coming," Papa said to Mama one night about a year later. Mama nodded soberly.

"I'd better oil the locks on the shutters."

On Friday morning, Papa did not go out with his cart, but closed all the shutters and secured them tightly. From the doorway, I watched the other Jewish families doing it, too. Only the Christian houses on the other side of the pond did not cover their windows.

"Devorah, I need to lock the door, too, mamaleh," Papa said. "It's not good for them to see you watching their procession."

"But why not, Papa?" I asked.

With a sigh, he sat down heavily in the darkened house and took me on his knee. "The Christians believe God had a son called Jesus Christ. Today is the anniversary of his death," he said. "It was the Romans who killed him, but the priest tells them it was the Jews. So they hate us today. Next week they will be good neighbors again."

Papa's face was dark, and I couldn't ask him any more questions. But I wondered why the priest told the villagers we'd killed the son of their god, and also how the villagers could change back and forth between hating us and being good neighbors. Were there other days when they would hate us, also? I decided to observe the villagers more closely, looking for a sign that would warn us that they were changing.

"Papa, here's a hole!" Nechama exclaimed. "I can see them."

Papa examined the chink in the shutters and said we could watch through it. Then he began reorganizing his boxes of wares while Mama lit a candle to do her sewing. Nechama and I took turns putting our eyes to the crack to watch the procession outside. The priest walked first, leading the way for a man carrying a huge cross, and the villagers followed, singing.

I didn't explain to Nechama why we weren't invited. Knowing that the marchers were busy hating Jews made me feel bad. But I did enjoy the sweet, somber singing. Was it all right to love the melody but not the words?

The man carrying the heavy wooden cross was neither young nor strong; he struggled as he stumbled up the hill. All the fit, healthy men had been taken to fight in the Great War. Papa was strong, but he hadn't had to go because his brother, Uncle Pinchas, was already in the army.

I remembered exactly when Uncle Pinchas had been conscripted to fight for the Czar. Sometimes my mind found the memory in the night and I couldn't stop myself from seeing his face, then Aunt Friedka's. When I started thinking about the big soldiers' faces, I rubbed my eyes with my knuckles to press the pictures away and huddled closer to Nechama's easy, light snoring.

Uncle Pinchas was taken on a cool Saturday afternoon the previous fall. I was visiting my aunt and uncle, nibbling on dried cherries and being careful not to drop any pits on the floor. Aunt Friedka's house was even tidier than our own. But it wasn't fair to compare, because it was hard to keep everything neat when there were two children and a mother at home all day, whereas Aunt Friedka and Uncle Pinchas both worked away from home. Aunt Friedka was one of the few Jewish women I knew who did that. She was very good with figures and the butcher hired her to keep his accounts, because he was better with a sharp knife than a chalk slate. That also gave Aunt Friedka the opportunity to buy certain cuts of meat that Jewish people weren't allowed to eat, and she would sell them to Christian villagers and make a little extra money. "Resourceful," Papa once called her, with approval in his voice. I wanted to be resourceful, too.

That particular Saturday I was waiting for Papa to walk past on his way home from synagogue, so that I could go with him. I'd saved a few dried cherries for Nechama, and I was sucking on the sour pit of the last one I'd eaten. Uncle Pinchas had not gone to pray because he had a cold; he was drinking hot tea.

Suddenly there was shrieking outside. Mrs. Leib came running down the lane, sobbing and flapping her apron. "The army is taking men from the shul! God help us, the soldiers are dragging men into their cart!" she wailed as she stumbled past.

We all ran to the door, and as Aunt Friedka opened it, we heard the sound of shouting and crying coming from the synagogue.

"Papa's at shul!" I exclaimed. The skin of my right eyelid started to jump up and down, and I pressed two fingers against it. "Who is taking men? What's happening?"

Aunt Friedka had a different man on her mind. In an instant, she shoved her husband back inside. "Quick, Pinchas, you have to hide. Maybe they'll go from door to door after the synagogue. Here! No, here, in the chest with the blankets. Hurry, Pinchas."

It seemed only a minute or two until we heard the noise of cartwheels rattling along the alley. Jews wouldn't be riding on the Sabbath, and none of the villagers would have reason to come this way, so it had to be the soldiers' cart. I prayed fiercely, digging my nails into my hand. "Make it go past, God. Don't let it stop."

The cart stopped right outside. "Here?" I cried.

Aunt Friedka glared at me warningly and hissed, "Shh! Drink your tea."

The sun was blocked out as big rough men pushed their way in through the low doorway and took up all the space. I shrank into my chair. They were so large, and there were three of them, all clad in greenish gray uniforms, stained and even ragged. The heaviest one seemed to be the leader. He brandished a grimy piece of paper and a stump of pencil.

"Move aside!" he shouted. "The Czar's army needs one more strong man from this village and the other Jews got away."

"My husband is not at home," said Aunt Friedka firmly, and she stood up right in front of the soldier. I squeezed my mug of tea so tightly that my fingertips were white.

With one burly arm, the soldier thrust her into a corner and she fell. A scream slipped out of my mouth. "You Jews are either at home or at your synagogue on Saturdays. Search the house, men."

I ran to Aunt Friedka as she got up from the floor, her mouth grim. She grasped my hand and we stood clutching each other while the men stomped around the room in their muddy boots. With loud crashes, they turned the bed and benches upside down. The house was small and it took only a few minutes until they noticed the chest.

"And what do the Jews keep in here?" one soldier shouted, throwing open the wooden lid with its heavy hinge. Aunt Friedka's hand tightened around mine.

Another giant soldier, with cloth puttees wound around the calves of his massive legs, tossed aside the top blankets and let out a guffaw. Then he leaned down and grabbed the body bent double inside. Uncle Pinchas's cap was knocked askew and his face was white with shock.

"Number seven," the leader announced, and he licked his stub of pencil and laboriously scribbled something on his paper. "Move him out. Next village."

With a shriek, Aunt Friedka snatched the blankets from the ground and ran after the soldiers. I ran right behind her.

"Pinchas, take the blankets. Pinchas, you will be cold."

Uncle Pinchas twisted and managed to grab the blankets from her as he was shoved into the back of the cart with the other Jews. In a flash, I scanned every face of the six men sitting stunned on the wooden bench, dust from the scuffle streaking their black Shabbes coats. No Papa, no Papa; they didn't have my papa.

Uncle Pinchas was the last in line, his face leaning anxiously toward his wife. "Friedka! I will be back! I will write as soon as I get there. Take care of yourself, Friedka!" Then we could no longer hear his voice as the cart rattled away from the village.

"Help! Mama, Papa, help!" I screamed as Aunt Friedka's body sagged and she sat down hard on the ground. With all my strength, I supported her shoulders. I was shaking like a leaf, but I managed to hold her until the neighbors ran to us. They shouted for Papa, and then I was in his arms.

About six months after Uncle Pinchas was conscripted, there was a sudden banging on our own door one afternoon. Nechama and I rushed to Mama's skirt and she pulled us behind her. Then she stood as if paralyzed. The knocking was repeated even more loudly; finally Mama stepped forward to open the door.

A stranger in a worn uniform thrust out an envelope. "Official business of the Czar," he announced importantly. Reluctantly, Mama took the envelope from him. He turned and strode off.

I drew in a sharp breath. It really was from the Czar: there was a big stamp showing his close-bearded head. Nechama reached out her hand and fingered the thick red sealing wax anchoring a piece of red ribbon. "The Czar sticks a ribbon on his letters," she said wonderingly.

"It's a letter for Papa from the army," Mama said dully. "Devorah, take Nechama outside and don't bother me now."

I didn't want to leave Mama. I wanted to stay with her and help her. And I wanted her to promise me that Papa would never leave us. But I led Nechama out very slowly. "Come on, Nechama, we have to go."

Outside everything felt different and strange. The forest nearby looked menacing, and the dried mud tracks worn by Papa's cart seemed to lead only one way, away from us. Nechama played little games in the dust while I sat on a tree stump and kept my eyes on the open doorway to the house. I could see that Mama did little work. Finally she just sat very still on the doorstep and waited for Papa to come home. Nechama stopped playing. We all sat.

Papa must have caught sight of us from a short distance, because he abandoned his horse and peddler's cart on the hill, and ran down. "Chanah! Chanah, what is it?" he shouted. She held out the letter silently. They hurried inside together and shut the door without a word to us.

Nechama and I sat in silence. The wind moaned in the forest. Then there was the sound of slow hoofbeats as Papa's old horse came clop-clopping steadily to our house and stopped.

"Soos!" I called out to him, grateful for any company. "You came home alone. Good boy, Soos." The big animal looked directly at me for a moment and snorted loudly through the tunnels of his black nostrils. I clucked and smiled at him nervously. I had never taken care of the horse before, but I had watched Papa many times. "Be brave, Devorah," I said aloud.

Walking to him slowly, I reached up high to take hold of the bridle. He snorted again, and I had to force the smile to stay on my face. What if he bites my hand? I thought. Or steps on my toes?

Soos didn't seem interested in me. He snuffled disappointedly at the empty feed bag hanging on the fence post, and then slurped at some water at the bottom of his trough. I wasn't quite seven yet, and I had to stretch up on my toes and strain to hook his reins over the fence post securely. Then I ran to the feed bin, pried up the heavy lid, and grabbed the tin cup lying inside. Filling it with grain, I carried it carefully over to the feed bag. I spilled only a little along the way, and some more when I poured it into the limp bag. By my third trip, the bag was bulging invitingly open and the horse lowered his head to push his big soft lips into the feed. When I was sure he was busy, I lifted the loop of the feed bag and hooked it over Soos's sweaty neck just as Papa did, keeping my fingers away from his huge teeth. I was spurred on by Nechama's look of silent admiration.

It was beyond my strength to unhook the wooden cart, and I couldn't manage to carry from the cart a pile of animal skins and two rolls of linen. But one by one I lifted out Papa's lighter baskets and placed them neatly outside the closed door of the house. "What's next?" I muttered. If I could find something else to do, I wouldn't have to think about Papa and the army.

"I'm thirsty," Nechama whined.

"That's it! Help me with the pump, Nechama," I ordered, and together we pulled on the handle and pumped and pumped until the small bucket was full. I knew I could carry just that small bucket and no more. I filled a dipper of cold water for Nechama, and then stumbled back and forth to the horse, pouring each bucketful as carefully as I could into his low trough. The horse drank gratefully, and I patted his steaming rough flank with new affection. "We did it, Soos," I said.

The door creaked. Head down, Papa emerged from the house. First he saw his goods stacked at the door, then he glanced up to see his horse fed and watered. I ran to him as his strained face turned pink with surprise and pride.

"My big girl. I see I can rely on you," he said, and he hugged me tightly.

I closed my eyes and breathed in his workday smell, loved even the pressure of his buttons against my cheek. Then Papa reached out to tousle Nechama's curls, and he sent us inside while he unhitched the cart.

After dinner, I lay awake. Papa and Mama were whispering and working together at the table. Keeping my eyes half-closed, I peeked toward the candlelight. Papa was writing laboriously on a piece of paper, reading a few words softly to Mama, then bending forward to write again. I fell asleep before they were finished.

The next day Papa went off to work as usual, but he and Mama seemed anxious and distracted. The same thing happened for many days after that. As weeks passed, though, Papa and Mama seemed less worried.

But I was not reassured. Questions twisted inside me. I wanted so badly to ask Mama. Each bedtime when she whispered the Shema with me at her side, looking out through the window at the silent village huddled in the moonlight, I felt the questions rising up, up, almost reaching my lips. And then at the last minute I pushed them down again. It would upset Mama to talk about what the letter had said. And the answer might be too hard for me to stand.

Finally, one night, the words exploded. "Is the army going to take Papa, too, Mama?"

There was silence. I couldn't bear to look up. Then Mama bent down and hugged me.

"No, we don't think so, Devorahleh." Her voice was

shaky, and she kept her face in my hair. "Papa wrote and told them that he and Uncle Pinchas are twins. If two brothers are twins, the army only takes one."

Relief filled me. I felt so light I could float. Papa was not going away, Papa was not going away. I slipped between Mama's dress and her apron, wound her apron tightly around me, and shivered with delight.

Later, as I drifted off to sleep, I wondered why I had never known before that Papa and Uncle Pinchas were twins. It's a good thing they are, I thought drowsily. Poor, poor Aunt Friedka.

# FROM PINSK TO WARSAW
## 1921

"**I**'m going with the nice man."

I stared at Nechama in shock. I had never heard my little sister state anything so strongly, never seen her so independent. We were standing in the hallway of the orphanage in Pinsk, the day after the man from Africa had arrived. In such a short time, she had latched on to his terrifying proposal.

"I'm going to Africa," Nechama repeated, her small fists clenched.

Then she moved closer and stared at me with her big, appealing eyes. "Please come with me, Devorahleh. I want you to come, too."

"And if I don't?" I asked, with real curiosity.

Nechama didn't hesitate for a moment. "I'm going," she repeated again, and then once more. "I'm going with that man to that new place."

My heart lurched. I sat down on a little bench nearby and tried to think. There was a long silence.

It wasn't as if I myself didn't feel drawn to Isaac Ochberg. He was warm and strong and gentle. But couldn't he see that going to Africa meant my old life was over? Once we sailed across the huge seas, we'd never come back, that was certain.

And where were we going? To a place where we knew no one and nothing, not even the language. I thought about the excited, frightened whispers I had heard coming from two older boys the previous night.

". . . lions and tigers," Shlayma said.

"Oh no," Itzik corrected him proudly. "The man told me there are no tigers in Africa."

"Well, lions and elephants, then," Shlayma conceded. "And what about cannibals? We might be eaten by cannibals."

There was a stunned silence.

"Or sold as slaves," Itzik offered.

"Or drowned at sea," Shlayma said, not to be outdone.

"I'm not scared," said a small boy's voice, and they turned to stare at little Yankel. "I'm going to drink the milk an' honey and get strong," he announced.

They looked at him in puzzlement, until Itzik let out a shriek of laughter. "He heard the man say Africa is a land of milk and honey like Palestine. What are you expecting, Yankel, rivers of warm milk?"

"And honey dripping from the trees?" Shlayma chimed

in mockingly.

They laughed wildly, their fears making them hysterical. Then Yankel burst out crying. "I want my milk an' honey. I want. Don't laugh. Stop laughing."

Eventually Mr. Bobrow heard the uproar and swooped in to comfort Yankel and order everyone to sleep.

After the other children had begun to snore, I slipped out of bed to stand alone at the window. I said the Shema, as usual, and my thank you to Aunt Friedka, as usual, and then it was time to talk. "Mama, I'm scared. I'm scared, Papa. I'm scared of—of—lions and cannibals and—Africa. If we go to Africa, how will we ever get home? I want to go home. But Panya Truda told us there was no one left. We can't live alone at home—among those people who— We have no place left in Poland. What's going to happen to us now, Papa? Mama?"

Outside, I could see an old man picking his way through the rubble in the street. He was looking for something in the moonlight, perhaps something from the past, from before everything collapsed, but he wasn't finding it.

Now, sitting on my little bench and facing Nechama's determination, I was being forced to decide: Europe or Africa? My little sister continued to stand, sturdily, very still, in front of me.

She looks like a stranger, I thought. What has happened to her since we left home?

I had never followed Nechama before; I had always

led. But if I wasn't sure about Africa, I was sure about something else. Mama would have said it, Papa would have said it, and I knew it in my heart: Wherever Nechama went, there went I.

Then came a long journey from Pinsk on a slow, dirty train to Warsaw, the biggest city in Poland. There were twelve orphans in our group: Nechama and I and four others from the orphanage in Pinsk—Itzik, Shlayma, Nechama's friend Malke, and little Yankel—plus six children, all girls, from an orphanage in Brest. None of us had ever been on a train before. The countryside moved across my eyes and disappeared. When I leaned forward to see where we had come from, I bumped my head on the smeared glass.

The train seats were worn through in places, and I kept trying to push away a metal spring that was poking through the old leather into my leg. Nechama was squashed beside me in the crowded compartment. "Isn't it wonderful that our own Mr. Bobrow is coming with us to South Africa?" I whispered to her.

"I asked him to," she murmured sleepily over the clacking of the wheels, her head rocking with the train's movement.

"Silly," I retorted. "He's not coming because you invited him. He wouldn't leave his work at the orphanage for that. He's coming because Mr. Ochberg is gathering two hundred children in Warsaw to take to South Africa, and he needs Mr. Bobrow's help taking care of us all."

"Two hundred," Nechama repeated, opening her eyes with interest for a minute. "Do you think there will be girls my age?"

I didn't bother to answer her question. Why did Nechama need more friends? Wasn't I enough for her?

But I did feel much better knowing that Mr. Bobrow would be with us all the way from the orphanage in Pinsk to the orphanage in South Africa. He was the person who had lifted us from the wooden cart when we arrived in Pinsk and led us to our iron cots. He was the one who had written down my name and Nechama's and those of our parents and our old village. He knew that much of my past. I turned to him, but he was talking with Isaac Ochberg.

"Right now it's Laya and Pesha I'm worrying about," Mr. Ochberg was saying. "I don't know how their eyes became so red and swollen so quickly, but it looks very contagious. If a health inspector gets on the train to check for diseases, he's sure to suspect trachoma. We'll be thrown off the train at the next station."

Instantly I was wide awake. Pressing my face against the glass, I began scanning each station platform carefully. And not very long after, I caught sight of a man wearing official-looking epaulets and a cap with a faded gold ribbon. There were many men in uniform in Poland, but this one hailed the train guard with a mixture of familiarity and authority before he swung himself up onto the train.

I turned to Mr. Ochberg, who was reading some

papers. "I think there's an inspector," I whispered. "He boarded the car behind us."

Mr. Ochberg and Mr. Bobrow glanced at each other.

"It could be," said Mr. Bobrow, pushing up his spectacles with an agitated gesture. "I'd better move Pesha and Laya forward. I'll take a few little ones to make us less conspicuous. Children, some of you must come with me quickly. Laya, carry baby Gittel. You, Pesha, take Yankel. Nechama, Faygele, and Braindel, follow me closely."

Nechama stood up obediently, and without hesitating I jumped up and stood next to her.

"Not you, Devorah," Isaac Ochberg began. "You stay here and—"

I turned to him, begging him with my eyes.

"Go ahead," he said gently. "You may go with your sister. Braindel, you stay here instead."

Braindel hurried back to her friend Rosha, looking relieved.

"Quickly, into the corridor," Mr. Bobrow urged.

We stood there swaying uncertainly for a moment, and then we heard a loud voice in the open doorway of the compartment right behind ours.

". . . authorized by our glorious new government to check for improper documents, contraband goods, and infectious diseases. I must ask . . ."

It *was* an inspector. For just an instant I felt proud that my guess had been right. Then fear snatched my breath and sucked it out of me. There was a determined hand on my back. Mr. Bobrow was moving us all along the corridor. Ten or eleven doors down, we reached the end of the train car and stood there, pretending to look out the windows.

"Stay here," Mr. Bobrow ordered quietly. "I'll go back and see how fast he's going. Talk to one another. Come on, talk happily. Don't look as if you're frightened."

My eyes widened. Was he really going to leave us there alone? Jews weren't safe on trains. Once I had heard Aunt Friedka tell a neighbor about thugs who boarded trains and threw Jews off the back while the train was still moving.

From behind me came a bright, high voice. Little Faygele was quick to assume her new role as an actress.

"And how are you doing, Miss Lehrman?" she asked cheerfully, turning to Nechama. "Are you enjoying the sunny weather?"

Nechama gaped, and then she responded to a not-so-subtle prod from Faygele. "Yes, thank you," she managed.

"Well, I'm fine, too," chimed in Yankel, not to be outdone. "And how is your arthritis?"

Laya and Pesha doubled up with wild, hysterical laughter, and Laya's baby sister, Gittel, laughed, too, as she watched them.

"Arthritis! Arthritis!" Pesha guffawed.

"That's what my mama used to say to Panya Netta," Yankel retorted loudly, his dignity offended.

Just one window away, two women frowned at us disapprovingly.

A moment later, Mr. Bobrow returned. "The inspector is taking a long time in each compartment," he said softly. "So we have time until he gets close to us. Maybe we'll reach a station by then. We can get off the train and run back along the platform until we're near our own compartment and get back on."

"What happens if we don't reach a station soon?" someone asked. Everyone looked back down the corridor anxiously.

I thought fast. "If he's taking so long in each compartment, we could slip past him and get back to Mr. Ochberg," I suggested.

Pesha's face turned pale. With her inflamed eyes, she looked like a sad clown wearing red-and-white makeup. "We'll have to walk so close to him," she said shakily.

"But he'll be talking to the people in the compartment, with his back to us," I pointed out.

"Let's do it!" Mr. Bobrow decided, pushing his spectacles up firmly. "I'll go first and warn you when we're getting close to the inspector. Whatever you do, don't look into the compartment where he's standing."

Fear was a rock in my chest as I followed Mr. Bobrow at a distance. Nechama pressed against my back. The other children fell in behind. Soon Mr. Bobrow gave an urgent wave, without turning around to us. I glanced back as we all quickened our steps. Laya had her head bent over baby Gittel, while Pesha kept her face toward the outer windows.

For a moment we heard the booming voice of the

inspector again. He was just beginning his speech in a new compartment.

"Attention, if you please. I am the inspector authorized by our glorious new government to . . ."

Out of the corner of my eye, I caught sight of his broad back. His gray uniform reminded me of the soldiers who had grabbed Uncle Pinchas. Panic forced bile from my stomach to my throat. I just knew that in a second or two the loud voice would be turned in our direction, a heavy hand would grab my shoulder. I heard Nechama whimper very softly, and I reached back to get hold of any part of her. My fingers brushed her sleeve and I held on tightly.

Ahead, Mr. Bobrow shoved a door aside. I felt him push me into a compartment and I stumbled inside with Nechama, the others right behind. Isaac Ochberg's face stared up at us, gray with worry. We were back in our own compartment, safe from the inspector.

"We were at the end—" Nechama burst out excitedly, but I squeezed her arm to silence her.

Two strangers were sleeping in the seats we had left vacant. Mr. Ochberg was signaling us with a quick pursing of his lips to be quiet.

Nechama subsided immediately. She, too, understands danger, I thought grimly. Mr. Ochberg and Mr. Bobrow told Braindel to give me her seat and squeeze in with Rosha. I took Nechama onto my lap. She was too big to fit comfortably, but we sat very close together, her back pressed against my chest.

Mr. Bobrow leaned over and patted my hand. "That was a good idea of yours, back in the corridor," he whispered softly. "Now get some sleep if you can."

I closed my eyes, still feeling Mr. Bobrow's approving pat. Papa used to pat me that way when he was proud of me. I felt proud of myself, and relieved, and still frightened, all mixed up together. But mainly I felt so, so tired. The train wheels called out a rhythm, "*Mama*, Pa-pa, *Mama*, Pa-pa, *Mama*, Pa-pa . . ." I let go and sank into the words.

## MAMA AND PAPA
### 1915–16

Weekday mornings in our village of Domachevo began with the sounds of Papa and big Soos outside.

"Stand still there, Soos," Papa murmured. "The cart is heavy today, yes?" There was the creak of the leather harness and the jingle of the metal bit as Soos tossed his head.

"Wake up, Nechama, Papa's leaving," I urged my sister, and we ran to the door in our long nightdresses to wave goodbye.

Papa's worn jacket stretched over his back as he bent to check the horse's hoof. Nechama and I giggled. Soos looked so funny balancing placidly on three legs with his surprisingly delicate hind limb tucked under Papa's arm, hoof pointing up to the sky.

"Bye, Papa, goodbye," we each called. Our papa always turned to blow kisses as he walked up the hill behind his peddler's cart. We caught the kisses in midair and blew them back until he was out of sight.

With a clang, Mama set down a bucket of icy water from the well. "Wash your hands and get the sleep out of your eyes," she ordered. Her own face was already clean, her hair groomed neatly, and her workday apron tied on tightly.

"Don't splash me, Devorah. I'm cold," squealed Nechama.

"Nechama didn't wash her eyes, Mama," I reported, drying my frozen fingers mischievously on Nechama's nightshirt.

"Devorah's wetting me, Mama!" Nechama cried.

Mama ignored our bickering. Shivering harder than we really needed to, we jumped back into our still-warm bed to pull on our clothes.

The door banged as Mama returned from the yard, where Tsigele, our goat, was tethered. She poured a frothing white ocean of goat's milk into our bowls. Wisps of steam rose into the air. I curved one hand around my bowl to catch the warmth and used the other to dunk boats of dark bread into my milk. Nechama copied me, except that she ate the sodden crusts with a greedy slurp.

Then Mama pushed up the sleeves of her cross-stitched linen blouse and began to prepare the day's food. Nechama had to pick garlic from the muddy vegetable patch outside the door, while I had to peel cold, knobby potatoes for soup. The peels mounted up high in a bowl for Tsigele, but still there always seemed to be more earth-brown unpeeled potatoes than skinned pale ones. At last Mama said we had helped enough and could go and play.

"Thank you, Mama!" I exclaimed, giving her a big hug. Then I grabbed Nechama's hand and hurried her along the muddy pathways between the thatched-roof houses. Our friends were already playing, giggling loudly as they crouched behind a higgledy-piggledy fence. We knew the game; we ran to hide with them.

"Shush, or the boys will hear us," Miriam warned.

Miriam was just being bossy: the boys couldn't possibly hear us from inside the large wooden synagogue, where they studied. Finally, a burst of whoops and yells announced that it was lunch hour, and the boys exploded out of the carved door. They came running down the lane like a herd of goats, long sidelocks flying under their caps.

"Go, girls!" Miriam ordered.

"Help, they'll run us down!" Nechama squealed as we scampered out into the lane ahead of the boys.

"Catch them!" the biggest boy commanded, and the herd moved as one into full chase.

"Help, help!" Miriam shrieked excitedly.

Soon I was in trouble. My legs were strong but short, and I was slowed by having to drag four-year-old Nechama along with me. The fastest boys were almost on my heels.

"Hurry, Nechama, run!" I said, panting.

Our crowd pelted around a corner of the narrow lane, and there was a yell from the front.

"The water carrier!"

His mouth hanging open, the water carrier stared dumbly at us. His chapped red hands clutched at the arched rod over his shoulder, from which hung two heavy buckets. The girls in front had just enough time to divide into two groups and run past on either side of him like the waters of the Red Sea. But for Nechama and me, and of course all the boys, there was not enough warning.

The buckets crashed to the ground. *Swoosh!* Water slopped all over the man's tattered black coat, which was tied at his waist with a rope. *Oof!* He grunted as he sat down hard in the mud. Shrieks of laughter burst from the boys and some of the bolder girls.

But the water carrier's face was purple with rage. "May you get warts on every finger! May your teeth rot and your noses bleed forever," he cursed as he got to his feet and righted his empty buckets. "I will tell your parents and they will beat you!"

The boys merely hooted and yelled and ran away, but I shivered as I kept picturing the spittle flying from the water carrier's mouth when he yelled. I had never done anything really bad before, never been in trouble. I crept through the rest of the day, then in the dark of night I composed my own prayer for the first time.

"Dear God," I whispered, "I'm sorry about the extra work we caused that poor man. I know my parents would never beat me, but please don't let the water carrier tell them what we did. I think I'd rather have a few warts, maybe four."

I made a deal with God for three warts the next night, and two the next, but there was no sign that the water carrier had made good on his promise, and after that I forgot to make my petitions. No hard little bumps appeared on my fingers, so I hid behind the fence outside the synagogue with the other girls again.

Sometimes, at the end of the day, when I was tired of playing, I climbed up the stepladder that led to our attic. Hiding there alone, I fingered my doll's golden hair. Maybe one day I could put some yellow dye in my own dark locks so that I could look just like the village girls in the Easter procession. Sunlight filtered in through the tiny, dusty window and sifted together with the smell of the hay and the sounds of geese honking, a cart creaking, a peasant shouting at his goat or his child or both.

The attic was a good place to dream. Nechama told me she dreamed of marrying a prince, even after I'd explained to her that princes were named Leopold or Vladimir, not Moishe or Yitzhak; in other words, princes were not Jewish. I had more practical dreams. When I grew up, I would have enough money to buy Papa a newer cart and a younger horse. Or, better still, I would order Papa to stop working altogether. A black velvet dress would bring out the beauty of Mama's hair. As for Nechama, I would save her from drowning in a lake, a bigger and much cleaner lake than the village pond. And I would do something so wise and brave to help the Jewish people that they would tell the story to their children and grandchildren.

As darkness fell, I heard Papa and his horse return slowly, and I tumbled down the ladder. Papa was stooping tiredly over the goods still in his cart, but his face curved into a smile when he saw me running to him.

"Here's my big seven-year-old," he said, and he lifted me high and tickled me.

I loved evening the best. From my seat in the kitchen, I could see into the only other room in our house, Mama and Papa's bedroom. It was completely filled by their bed and a large carved cupboard, which stood near the window and held all our clothes. Nechama and I slept on a small bed in one corner of the kitchen. The wood walls were roughly plastered inside and felt damp most of the year, while the window had strips of old cloth squeezed into the frame to close the gaps. But our family sat in the evenings near the big blackened stove, on wooden benches on either side of the table, and we were warm together.

"Mama, those cheese kreplach were almost too good," Papa said, rubbing his stomach, with a wink at us. The cheese was goat cheese, kept cool in the musty root cellar below the house. Mama had a clever trick to make it. First she poured goat's milk into a bag made from clean, thin cloth. Then she hung the bag on a very long string that stretched from a rafter to just above the kitchen table. Cloudy water dripped through the cloth into a bowl, and then came the magic: what was left inside the bag was the creamy white cheese I loved.

Most nights after supper, Papa lit a candle on the table and bent his high, balding forehead and his long sidelocks over a scrap of paper. I heard his low mutter as he counted the coins he had earned from his peddling that day: "Eyns, tsvey, dray—one, two, three . . ." Mama listened silently as she braided my thick hair for bed. Nechama's hair was so curly that Mama kept it cut short and needed only to comb it a few times. I was jealous as I watched her twirl Nechama's light tendrils admiringly between her fingers. But the highlight of the evening was coming. When Papa was done with his accounting, he would be ready to tell us stories. Papa knew the best stories in the world.

Some of the stories were exciting and happy: about my namesake, the first Devorah, who became the judge and leader of all the Jews. And about Sarah, who finally had a baby when she was ninety years old and called him a name that meant "Laughter." But some tales were scary. A woman named Judith gave an evil general so much wine that he fell asleep, and then cut off his head. In Devorah's time, there was a woman, Jael, who killed an enemy leader by knocking a tent peg through his temples as he slept in her tent. How did she hold the tent peg and swing the mallet hard at the same time? What would have happened if she hadn't got the peg in all the way? I thought, shivering.

For nights, the gory story went around and around in my head. I tried different solutions to Jael's problem. Perhaps a strong two-handed blow with the mallet, without a tent peg at all, would have done the job. Or maybe a large metal half circle—the swinging handle detached from a cooking pot, for instance—could have been leaned delicately around the sleeping general's neck, then quickly hammered into the ground, trapping him. Yes, I would be really brave if the Jewish people faced terrible trouble again, I finally decided.

Over a thousand Jews lived in my shtetl of Domachevo, but only about a hundred Christian villagers. I recognized many of them from the weekly farmers' market held next to the village pond.

Market day in Domachevo was Thursday. Nechama and I didn't like it much. There was such a clamor of people shouting out their wares and arguing over prices. And we hated the smells of glassy-eyed fish and rotting vegetables.

"What do we need, Mama?" I asked as we reached the first stall.

"Eggs and wheat. Apples. And nuts, if they're a good price," Mama replied. Even Mama seemed louder and more aggressive at the market. Nechama and I watched closely while she bargained in the mixture of Polish and Yiddish used between Jews and Christian villagers.

First Mama asked, "How much?"

The peasant gave her a price in a rough voice, as if he didn't care whether she bought or not.

Mama reacted with shock. "That's much, much too high!"

Then the peasant raised his arms to the sky and swore, "Mary, Mother of God, you know that my prices are lower than I can afford! You see how my children are starving!"

His children, who looked poor but not starving, stared at us. We shrank against Mama's skirts. Mama turned away, but the peasant called her back with a beckoning finger. Leaning forward, he volunteered a lower price.

Mama offered less than his figure, and again the peasant swore, "Mother Mary, I cannot go so low!" Then he countered immediately with another slight reduction in his price.

Mama nodded. She counted out some coins; the peasant handed over the produce. Mama placed her purchase carefully into the center of her shopping cloth and knotted the cloth into a bundle. Then she and the peasant parted with a polite farewell.

"Mama, why do that man and his children . . ." I asked one day as we walked home from the market. "Why do they look at us as if we're . . . strange?"

Mama snorted. "Ignorant peasant. He can't even read and write like your papa can."

That didn't answer any of the questions in my head. But I knew how important it was to be able to read and write. Mama respected learning above everything else. Sometimes she called me to her side and gave me a little basket covered with a clean linen cloth.

"Devorahleh, take these hot potatoes to the shul.

Something to fill the students' bellies. No one can study the whole day on only glasses of tea with sugar."

All of the boys and a few of the men studied at the synagogue the entire day. The tall wooden building stood proudly at the center of the village. I glanced around for my friends as I walked up to the heavy door, hoping the other girls would see me entering the important building on a day that wasn't even Shabbes.

Inside the entrance hall, I had to stop for a few minutes until I could see my way in the dimness. A babble of male voices seeped from under the classroom door—high boys' voices singing the same aleph bet I was learning with Papa, as well as deeper men's voices chanting in singsong.

In a moment the rabbi shuffled out of the sanctuary carrying several worn books. His beard drifted like white clouds over his chest. "What is it, mamaleh?" he asked kindly.

I began to stammer with shyness, but I held up my basket and said what I'd come to say. "Hot potatoes, Rabbi. From my mama, Chanah Lehrman. For those who are studying."

The rabbi smiled. "A good woman," he said. "You should grow up to be like your mama." Then he patted my cheek, looking quietly into my eyes. "A sheyn ponim," he murmured.

I blushed and looked down. Not too many people said I had a pretty face. Certainly not when I was with Nechama.

The rabbi shuffled away, smoothing his beard again and again with a shaky hand, and I slipped silently through the open door into the sanctuary. In that solemn place, I stared at the painted murals on the walls. There were marvelous scenes from the Torah and pictures of vines and fantastical animals and birds. No pictures of God, but mountains and clouds where I thought He might be hidden. I lingered as long as I dared.

Mama's dream was for Papa to study here in the synagogue all day. "Or at least to say your morning prayers with the other men," she would say wistfully.

But Papa said he needed to begin his traveling while it was still dark. "I say my morning prayers as I walk next to the cart. God is also awake early," he said, smiling at me.

Mama shook her head. "With your brain, Bzalel . . . If you just had more time to study the Torah."

Silly Mama, I thought. Papa knows all the stories in the Torah already. There isn't a better storyteller than Papa.

The best day for stories was Shabbes. On Shabbes, Papa didn't have to work and Mama also rested. Shabbes was a whole night and a whole day long, from Friday evening at dusk until Saturday evening at dusk. Preparations began on Friday morning, when Nechama and I woke to the sight of Mama braiding bread—not the huge quantity of rough, brown wheat and rye bread that she baked on Sundays to last the whole week, but two loaves of fine white challah.

The cholent for Saturday lunch, with its beans and

potatoes, was also cooked on Friday, and then it was sent over to the home of Panya Truda, our nearest Christian neighbor. Panya Truda kept it warm for us because Jews are not supposed to light a fire on Shabbes.

At Friday night dinner, dressed in my embroidered blouse with my wavy hair allowed to fall freely instead of being pulled back tightly from my face, I felt like a princess. And how handsome Papa looked as he sat at the head of the kitchen table. The table wore a white linen cloth, and Papa wore his black Shabbes coat. He sang the blessing over the sweet red wine and the challah in his deep voice. Mama was queen for the night, sitting calmly on the bench instead of rushing around to serve us. She wore her best black dress and the pearl necklace that had been her marriage dowry and was her only jewelry.

When we returned home from synagogue on Saturdays at noon, Mama sent us to Panya Truda to fetch the cholent for our lunch. One Saturday I heard some Christian children shout Polish words that Nechama didn't understand yet. The next week I decided to go alone.

"Say hello nicely to Panya Truda and give her this ribbon with my thanks," Mama instructed me.

Silently I took the ribbon.

"Let's go," Nechama said.

"No," I said firmly, turning away. "I'll go alone." Then I hurried out the door before there was time for questions.

Slowly I walked down the road and around the village pond. Only about twenty-five houses in Domachevo were owned by Christians, and they were clustered together away from the Jews. So far, so good: no little blond boys or girls played in the mud at the edge of the pond.

I knocked at the first door on the other side of the pond. Panya Truda, who washed laundry for my mama each week, opened it with a little child in her arms. She always seemed tired and busy, but she greeted me kindly.

"My thanks to your mother for the pretty ribbon," she said. "It is no trouble for us to keep your Sabbath meal warm."

"We thank you, Panya Truda," I said very politely.

I placed the pot of cholent into my cloth-lined basket and turned to hurry home, quickly, before— Too late. The children were gathering at the pond, waiting for me to pass by. I breathed more shallowly.

"What you got?" a big boy shouted, pointing at my basket. "Give us a little. You Jews have got a lot."

"I don't want any of her stew. Jew stew smells bad!" a girl yelled in return.

Head up, head up, I told myself as jeers of laughter cracked around me. Just keep going. I kept walking.

Suddenly the big boy somersaulted right across my path. His face flashed past mine and for a moment it was the face of the soldier who had dragged out Uncle Pinchas. "Aai!" I cried out in panic.

"Scared her!" he boasted.

My heart was sore from pounding. Look straight ahead. Just look straight ahead. Anger started to mingle with my fear.

"Jew girl, stew girl, smelly Jew-and-stew girl," someone sang, and the others joined in.

I squeezed the handle of the basket until the straw bit into my skin, but I didn't start crying. Stupid, ignorant peasants! I yelled at them in my head. You don't even know how to read. I would never cry in front of you.

The jeers and shouts followed me around the curve of the pond. "She's getting away!" "Grab her basket!" "We'll get you next time!"

They wouldn't dare touch me now. Forty more steps, I told myself through clenched teeth. Thirty more steps; just twenty now; ten . . .

And I reached the safe encampment of Jewish houses. A glance behind told me the children had lost interest. They were grouped together throwing stones into the pond. I muffled a sob. Putting the cholent down for a moment, I bent over at the pump and scrubbed my face and hands vigorously. That would explain my burning cheeks. Then I went inside. Mama and Papa never knew how frightened I was to collect the cholent, and I never took Nechama with me again.

Every Saturday after lunch, Papa gave me a short lesson. He was teaching me to read the Hebrew letters used for both Yiddish and Hebrew. Mama knew the morning and evening prayers by heart, but she could barely read Hebrew. "I want you to know more than your mother," Mama told me. "Here are some gooseberries to give you strength to learn." I enjoyed the berries, but I didn't really need them. I loved learning with Papa.

Then, after the lesson, Papa took Nechama and me for a walk through the forests. Domachevo was surrounded by pine forests on the banks of the long Bug River. We often wandered through the thickly wooded cemetery on the outskirts of the town, looking at the wooden grave markers carved and painted with pictures. Each painting had a meaning, and Papa could decipher most of the stories for us. The saddest painting was my favorite. It was a picture of a Shabbes table, laid with bread and wine and ready for the mother to bless the lights. But there were only two candles in the five-branched candlestick, and they were unlit.

"Tell us the story again, Papa. Where are the other candles?" we asked as we all settled down in the long grass.

"This woman buried here had five children," Papa explained, "but only two survived. And then the mother died. But her spirit still lives, especially on Shabbes."

The painting was starting to blister, worn by rain and wind. I traced the colors gently with my fingertips.

"These pictures are getting fainter, Devorahleh," Papa remarked.

"Yes, see, the table is wearing away on one side. What will happen when we can't see them anymore?" I asked.

"People forget," Papa answered. "That's the way the world is. One day the stories of these people of Domachevo will be forgotten."

I felt a cold shiver rake my back. How could stories be

forgotten? How could people and their lives be forgotten?

"No, Papa!" I cried. "I will remember even when I can't see the paintings." I didn't know whether Papa believed me. I stood up so that he would know this was important. "I want to make a vow, Papa."

"A vow is a serious matter, Devorahleh," Papa said, without a hint of a smile. "Are you sure you want to make a vow?"

"Yes, Papa, I am sure." My voice sounded unnaturally loud. Nechama glanced up at me for a moment, then skipped off to pick wild poppies.

I pulled myself up tall. "I vow," I said slowly. "I vow before God and before my papa that I will always remember our stories."

There was silence in the cemetery. Then Papa stood up with a sigh. He put an arm around me and held me close.

"Your papa is very proud of you, Devorah," he said seriously. "My heart is full of pride. But my head worries about you. Now that you have vowed, you must remember. But there are different ways of remembering, my child. Hard ways and easier ways. I hope you will find an easier way."

I didn't understand. How could there be hard and easy ways of remembering? Either you remembered, and that was good—or you didn't, and that was bad.

But Papa had turned toward my sister. "Nechamaleh," he called to the little girl moving lightheartedly among the graves. "It is time for us to leave."

# THE WAIT IN WARSAW
## 1921

I woke up from a dream of home to find that the long journey from Pinsk was over: our train was pulling into the huge, bustling railway station in Warsaw. The ornate ceiling was so high above the noisy crowds that pigeons nested confidently in its eaves, swooping down to exit through the great doors. I followed Mr. Ochberg and Mr. Bobrow in a daze as they led us in pairs through the cobblestone streets to the only shelter Mr. Ochberg had been able to rent, a battered old schoolhouse at 28 Sliska Street.

There Nechama and I were assigned iron cots next to each other, with old mattresses leaking straw.

"I'm cold. The wind is coming right through those broken windows," Nechama complained.

"Well, at least we don't have to lie on the ground," I said, pointing at some mattresses that were placed on the floor.

Over the next few weeks, the rooms became more and more crowded as children arrived in small groups. We gathered around each time to see the arrivals. I scanned the faces for someone from the past, even though I knew there was no one left. Nechama hoped to find new friends.

"Welcome, welcome." Mr. Ochberg beamed. He sounded relieved, even though he looked exhausted. "Here you will be safe until the entire group of two hundred children has gathered, and then we can all travel on to South Africa."

There wasn't much more than this simple welcome to offer the newcomers. There was very little food, hardly any coal to heat the rooms, and no clothing. Medicine for Laya's and Pesha's eyes had to be bought on the black market. After years of war, famine, and sickness, the city of Warsaw was depleted.

On one of our daily walks through the city streets, Mr. Bobrow stopped to commiserate with a man wearing a yarmulke on his head who was boarding up his small bakery.

"No flour means no bread for my customers," the baker said sadly. "We're going to live with my wife's family until my brother sends money from America for us to move to the New World. Who can survive in Poland these days?"

I peered into the bakery as I listened to the men talk. In a huge basket on the floor were stacks of empty flour bags made out of strong, white cloth. Neatly folded, they reminded me of something. Yes, they looked almost like the linen Papa used to sell. Could we use them?

I tugged at Mr. Bobrow's sleeve. "What is it, sad one?" he asked. I couldn't talk aloud in front of the stranger, so I reached up to whisper into Mr. Bobrow's ear. His face brightened as he listened and he gave me a soft pat on my cheek before turning back to the baker.

When we returned to the schoolhouse a little while later, the bigger boys were carrying large bundles tied with string. Their faces and arms were ghostly, coated with white powder.

"What do you have there?" asked Mr. Ochberg when they dropped their load to the ground and clouds of white swirled around us. Suddenly I pictured the drifts of white feathers on the Night of the Burning. Feathers expelled and scattered, drifting and lost. I shuddered.

"Flour sacks!" Mr. Bobrow answered triumphantly. "There is so little flour that the bakery nearby no longer needs its flour sacks. The owner gave them to us for free." He pushed up his spectacles and left a white smudge on the glass.

"And how will empty flour sacks help us?" asked Mr. Ochberg. "We need the flour that should be inside them."

With a dramatic gesture, Mr. Bobrow flourished one of the sacks in the air and then wrapped it around his middle like a skirt. "Voilà!" he cried. "An apron!"

"We're going to make clothes!" a big boy called Zeidel said, snatching up a bag and pressing it against his body.

"Shirts! Skirts! Blouses!"

Another boy took mincing steps in an imaginary skirt, flicking a bag flirtatiously. Little Yankel was slotted into a bag by Zeidel and Shlayma and swung high as he squealed in excitement. Mr. Ochberg needed two big sacks to stretch all the way around his middle. Flour flew in the air, coating us all in a layer of white.

Something twitched at the corners of my lips, the memory of a smile.

"Enough, enough! Children, we have work to do," Mr. Bobrow called finally. He divided us into work groups: to shake out the flour sacks, sweep the floor, and find strong needles and thick thread.

As I hurried past the two men, Mr. Bobrow pulled me over for a moment and turned me to face Mr. Ochberg. "It was Devorah's idea. She realized we could make clothes out of them. Wasn't that resourceful?"

Resourceful. That's what Papa had called Aunt Friedka. My chest stretched with pride.

That evening we cut and sewed in the biggest classroom. I edged as close to the adults as I could. It made me uneasy to see Mr. Ochberg sitting still with his eyes closed and his face pale. Mr. Bobrow must have noticed, too. He handed Mr. Ochberg a glass of tea, which he stirred silently for a while.

"Thank you, Alexander," Mr. Ochberg said. "I'm worn out from the endless trips to the consulate to have the travel documents stamped. And every day I worry about finding enough food for these children. If you weren't here, I don't think I could do this."

Mr. Bobrow laughed gently. "You would manage, Isaac," he replied.

I nodded to myself. Mr. Ochberg could do anything; of course he would manage.

Mr. Bobrow continued. "When I was sent to Pinsk to help the Jewish war orphans, I thought my head would burst. Before the war, my life had been so well organized. As a chemist in the sugar factory, I had a quiet office with all my equipment lined up neatly and my hours set from eight to five." He let out a little sigh.

"Then I was in hell. War, revolution, typhus, pogroms—they raged outside our three orphanages. And all I could think about was how to buy some milk to add to the children's diet of potatoes, potatoes, potatoes. But occasionally a box with tins of cocoa and condensed milk arrived from America. Enough to make weak chocolate milk for everyone. The children's chocolate smiles lit up the dining room. Then I wasn't tired anymore."

My fingers sewed familiar stitches while I wondered about "condensed milk." What could that be? Did it come from goats or cows or some other animal altogether?

I snipped off my last thread and stood up to tie the apron around my waist. There was a large piece of mirror propped up in the front hall, and I slipped out to stand in front of it. Well, you couldn't tell that it used to be a couple of flour bags—it was clean and very white and the folds hung well. Mama would have been proud of my sewing. I twirled around, stopping as I saw Itzik watching me with a smile.

"You look just fine, Devorah."

I blushed furiously; even my ears felt aflame. "Thank you," I muttered, and hurried back to the classroom. In case he was still watching, I pulled out an old slate board and scribbled a few English words over and over again, as if I were really concentrating on our homework.

Mr. Bobrow spoke nine languages, including English. Every day he found time to give us English lessons. Big and small children were at the same level: we squeezed into the old school desks and repeated the strange words together.

In the evenings before we went to sleep, Mr. Bobrow displayed yet another talent: he played the ukulele. One song was serious rather than lilting and merry. Mr. Bobrow told us it was the English anthem and we should always stand at attention when we sang it. I couldn't make any sense of the words, but I sang it softly over and over to myself until I knew it by heart.

> "God sayr our gracious King . . .
> Long to ray ober us
> God sayr our King."

One day I heard a tremendous knocking on the front

door. I looked around wildly for help. I'd heard that kind of knocking before. When the man in the uniform delivered Papa's letter from the Czar, the letter that caused such fear in our house, he had knocked just like that. "Mr. Bobrow! Mr. Ochberg!" I shouted.

But the delivery was a happy occasion this time: two big cases and then two more. They kept coming, until sixteen large boxes blocked the entrance. Nechama and her friends leapfrogged from case to case.

"Open them, open them! They must be for us."

They really were for us, packed with secondhand clothing by the Jews in South Africa. We burrowed into the heaps of clothes, fighting to grab the warmest coats and the prettiest skirts.

"Look, Nechama," I marveled. "Instead of buttons up the back, this dress has a metal thing that goes up and down."

"It's like a tiny train . . ." Nechama began.

"Racing along tiny greased tracks," Itzik exclaimed.

"That, children, is a new device called a zip," Isaac Ochberg explained, laughing at our amazement. But I also saw him wiping away tears as he read to Mr. Bobrow the letters of support he found inside the boxes.

The next time a man came to our door with a big box was different again. The small children watched him with puzzlement, but I just smiled quietly. I know what he's carrying, I thought. They don't know, but I do. I fingered the photograph in my pocket, remembering the day long ago in my village when a man carrying a box had pulled out a smaller black box. He had handled the small box very, very carefully. From it had come a photograph.

"Shoo!" the man in Warsaw admonished some children who had edged closer. "Move away! Don't bump me." With great self-importance, he unfolded three tall metal legs into a triangle and attached the small box to the top corner. Then he hung a trailing black cloth over the long-legged box with a grand flourish and, without even a goodbye, climbed right under the cloth himself. His large bottom stuck out the back.

"Hee, hee!" A couple of children giggled. "Peep-oh! We can see you."

"Be polite," Mr. Bobrow said reprovingly, nudging his glasses into place as he hurried up to the crowd. "This man is a photographer. He uses that cloth to keep the light out of his camera. He's going to take photographs of you for your passports. Now, no pushing. I'll divide you into groups: twenty children in each photograph."

I searched quickly for Nechama and squeezed my way through the line to reach her. Sisters should be in the same photograph.

Faygele, the little actress from the train, sat in front of us for the photographs. Her straw mattress was next to ours at night. Faygele was a chatterbox. "I love Mr. Ochberg," she had whispered to me one night after Nechama fell asleep. "Some of us call him Daddy Ochberg now. He's taking us across the ocean."

"Yes," I replied briefly. I didn't feel like talking, but Faygele was not easily put off.

"I'm frightened of the ocean, Devorah. And of Africa. Aren't you frightened of Africa?"

"Yes," I said again. If Faygele was frightened, why was she so cheerful all the time? Her busy chatter was as silly as Nechama's childish giggles.

"But I said yes right away when he asked me to come with him," Faygele remembered. She sat up on her mattress and leaned closer to me, her eyes shining. "Don't you think I was brave?"

"We're all either brave or crazy," I muttered. "And there's no turning back now." I wasn't going to tell her that I lay awake for hours at night, bargaining with God, begging my parents, trying with all my might to go back in time to our life before. But when I saw little Faygele's puzzled eyes, I felt guilty. "Yes, you were brave," I said.

Each night, Nechama would grow quiet as darkness fell. She refused to lie on her own mattress and would climb under my blanket and curl into my arms. I loved those moments when she'd show how much she needed me. Often she awoke shuddering and trembling from nightmares, her body damp with perspiration.

"Big knife," she whimpered one night, clinging to me. "He had a big knife . . . Aunt Friedka, heavy . . ."

"Shh, shh, it'll be all right," I whispered, stroking Nechama's twining curls. "I'll sing Papa's song if you want. Shh, shh." I sang the old Yiddish lullaby softly, until I felt

Nechama's tense body relax. Her lips parted in quiet, even breathing. I breathed quietly, too, feeling satisfied for a while. Only I knew how to take care of Nechama, how to soothe my sister. The nights were long, but we were together.

In the mornings, however, Nechama awoke as cheerful as a bird, while I lay heavy and numb. After breakfast we had English classes, and then Nechama went off with Malke from Pinsk and her new little friend, Jente. I felt as if my strength went with her, leaving me limp and drained. Mainly I sat on my little iron cot, feeling tired down to my very bones, staring first at my photograph and then out of the window at the weak sun or the gray rain. Once or twice, Mr. Ochberg came over to lift my chin and look worriedly into my eyes, but I was too weary to wonder why.

The only part of the day I looked forward to was lunch with Madame Engel. Regina Engel was a well-known and generous Jewish widow who owned a large restaurant in Warsaw. She had thick, very wavy hair like mine, strong black eyebrows, and a handsome straight nose. She held herself upright and ruled her restaurant like a general. Every day we received a message from her telling us when it would be convenient for us to come for lunch, either before or after the rush of her usual customers. Then two hundred of us would line up and walk in neat pairs through the tree-lined cobblestone streets to the restaurant.

On our walks, I stared at the grand buildings and

carved marble monuments, which alternated with piles of stone and rubble left by the war. On almost every corner, women and children as thin and sick as Mama had been begged for coins. I remembered Mama's shrunken thighs, her belly swollen with emptiness, the dry paper-thin skin stretched over her bones. I couldn't do anything for her. And I couldn't do anything for these people.

Once or twice we saw people in fur coats, too, stepping from their carriages into stately homes.

"I wonder what they do behind those doors," I whispered to Nechama.

"Eat, of course. And dance with their friends," she replied with certainty.

The first time we visited Madame Engel's restaurant, we were all silent throughout the meal. A weekday seemed like Shabbes in that great, majestic room, with snowy tablecloths cascading to the ground, silver candelabra, and red velvet curtains as soft as the Torah cover before the Night of the Burning. Waitresses in ruffled aprons moved quietly in the hushed atmosphere. Something on the ceiling caught my eye and I stared. Painted up there were fat baby boy angels without any clothes on at all. I quickly looked down again at the food, thick lentil soup and bread. Afterward came rolled-up cabbage leaves stuffed with potatoes and onions. Everything was tasty, and the helpings were generous, too.

One lunchtime, I saw Isaac Ochberg point me out to Madame Engel and then whisper into her ear. I froze.

What had Mr. Ochberg said? What had I done to make myself conspicuous?

A few moments later, Madame Engel glided straight toward me like a ship.

"You will stay at my restaurant a bit longer today, little one," she said in a firm but kind voice. "Come and sit with me in my kitchen. I want you to taste a new recipe I am trying out. You will help me."

I flushed red, but found myself standing up and following her. It was not possible to say no to Madame Engel. And somehow I didn't really want to. I began eating my lunch in the kitchen every day and then staying there for a couple of hours. Madame bustled around, giving the maids rapid-fire orders.

"Quickly, wash all those children's bowls. Maria, you dry and put them away—not so high up, Maria, we'll need them again tomorrow. Good, now let's hurry up with the regular customers' dinner. We have one large party arriving in thirty minutes. Gerda, set the big table at the back with the best silver. Don't forget to light the candles."

The kitchen was many times bigger than my entire old home, scrubbed spotlessly clean, gleaming with copper pots and towering samovars. Two huge stoves made the air warm and steamy. I sipped my soup slowly just outside the bustle, at a tiny table set up especially for me. "What do you think, mamaleh? Too salty? Too much onion?" Madame would ask. Sometimes she would stroke my cheek as she passed.

It was all simple food because there was little to be bought at the market, but everything she made tasted delicious to me.

Why did she choose me? I asked myself again and again. At first Mr. Ochberg pointed me out to her for some reason I don't understand, but since then she has seemed to like me more than the other girls. She asks my opinion as if she really cares what I think. Even Mama never did that.

Once Madame stopped bustling around the kitchen and looked at me as I watched her. Her heavy dark brows relaxed for a moment and she smiled. "Such eyes," she murmured. "Huge dark eyes with the whole world in them." Then she shook her head and strode back to the big stove. I wondered what it was that she'd seen in my eyes.

How good Madame was. How quickly I grew to love her with all my heart. At night I had long fantasies that she would let me stay in her sweet-smelling kitchen forever—with Nechama, too, of course. We would remain in Poland and learn how to help her in the restaurant, and then we wouldn't have to move to that strange, frightening land: Africa.

# THE BEGINNING OF THE BAD TIME
## 1916–19

The bad time in my home began when I was about seven, on the morning Uncle Pinchas came back. That should have been the happiest moment for our family, but it turned out to be the beginning of the end.

One Shabbes in fall, Nechama and I slept at Aunt Friedka's house.

"Stay with your aunt this Shabbes," Mama had told us. "She's lonely."

Very early on Saturday morning, Aunt Friedka, Nechama, and I were all asleep together in the big bed. Suddenly we were awakened by the loud clatter of a cart stopping outside the door.

"Your man is home," a rough voice shouted in Polish. "Come and get him."

I reached for my aunt, but my fingers touched empty sheets. Aunt Friedka was already out of bed, at the door. As if even in her sleep she had been waiting a year for this moment. I pushed sleepy Nechama aside and jumped out of bed, too. I heard the clopping of hooves and the rattle of uneven wheels as the cart continued on its way.

I stood blinking at the door. Uncle Pinchas? It couldn't be. Aunt Friedka was leaning over a broken wreck of a man lying on the ground, dirty, gray-faced, and still. Still except for the bubbling, stuttering wheezes that seemed to come from a wet place deep inside him.

"Easy, easy, you're home now," Aunt Friedka was murmuring again and again, her voice surprisingly calm and low. But when she turned to me, I fell back a step. Aunt Friedka's face was white, her eyes empty.

"Send Nechama for your parents and the barber," she ordered. "Then help me carry your uncle into the house."

I fled inside. "Nechama! Nechama! Wake up!" I shouted, and pulled her roughly to her feet. "Run home and get Papa!" She stared at me, her mouth open. "Run!" I shouted again, pointing through the open door. "They brought Uncle Pinchas back. He's— Go get Papa."

Still in her nightdress, she scampered outside, gaped at the figure lying on the ground at Aunt Friedka's feet, peered back at me in horror, and disappeared in the direction of home.

"Take his legs," Aunt Friedka ordered.

I couldn't touch that filthy, wheezing bundle. I had to. I couldn't. Then I saw his hand outspread on the ground. It was Uncle Pinchas's long, slim hand. The last time I saw him, that hand had held hot tea, when Uncle Pinchas was

71

master in his own home on another Shabbes morning a lifetime ago. I crouched down and lifted Uncle Pinchas's cracked boots as firmly as I could, while Aunt Friedka carried him by the shoulders. Together, we managed to lift him onto the high bed.

"Chanah's gone for the barber," Papa said as he ran in the door. The nearest doctor was more than a day's journey away and no one in the village could afford his fees, anyway. So we had to rely on the village barber.

Papa and I struggled to take off the boots, while Aunt Friedka began unwrapping something stiff and mud-soaked that had been wound around Uncle Pinchas. One single sob broke from her. "It's the blanket I gave him. When they took him away."

There was a cough at the door as the barber announced his arrival. Lifting his bulging leather bag of medicines onto the table, he squinted at the long names on the labels.

Mama followed him in. "Go home," she ordered me. "Go home and look after Nechama. She's very scared."

I'm scared, too, I wanted to whisper. I don't want to be alone. But Mama was busy boiling hot water to heat the barber's poultices. I walked out very slowly—maybe she'd change her mind and let me stay with her. She didn't. Nechama, it was always Nechama who had to be taken care of.

Late that night, I heard Papa talking bitterly to Mama. "There's no medicine that will help Pinchas. The German gases eat up a man's lungs. That's how they poison thousands of men as they lie in the trenches."

Mama's voice was tearful. "The army didn't want him any longer," she said. "He was already half dead, so they sent him home. Your poor sister."

I fumed silently. When I'm big, I'm going to organize the women of the village to hide our men in the forest, or in the cemetery maybe. I'll never let them steal our men when I'm big.

The next day I was allowed to help Mama and Aunt Friedka nurse their patient, while Nechama played outside. Uncle Pinchas lay on the bed heaving for breath, his eyes always on Aunt Friedka. Even when she walked across the room to heat a brick in the stove and wrap it in a cloth to warm his feet, he strained to see her. Mama said he must have longed for the sight of his wife for so long that he dared not let her disappear for even a moment. He watched her for six days and then he had to let go. He died with his eyes open, looking at Aunt Friedka.

"Aai," Aunt Friedka gasped. "Aai, aai, aai."

When the members of the Burial Society came to take away the body, she cried. I couldn't bear to see that; not strong Aunt Friedka. Mama had her arms around her and I threw my arms around both and squeezed with all my might.

But it was the only time I ever saw Aunt Friedka cry. After that, she closed her face and straightened her back, and she stayed closed and straight until the Night of the Burning.

Some months after Uncle Pinchas died, I glanced up from my plate at dinner and caught a strange expression on Mama's and Papa's faces as they watched Nechama and me eat. Their own plates were scraped empty, and I realized suddenly and certainly that they were hungry. I looked down again right away; they wouldn't want me to notice. It was true: there was less and less food in our house. Mama didn't buy fish except for Shabbes and there was never any fruit. Potatoes weren't merely a part of the meal anymore: potatoes were usually the entire meal, with goat's milk to wash them down.

Then one sad day, Mama, Nechama, and I took Tsigele to the marketplace, taking turns leading the goat with the leash for the last time. A butcher from a nearby town bought her after some hard bargaining with Mama, and we returned home silently. No more friend Tsigele, no more cheese. After that, we walked to the dairyman's barn at the edge of town each morning, and Mama bought just a cup of milk for Nechama and me to share.

"Thanks be to God we have saved a little, Chanah," Papa said softly one night. "The peasants do not know how to save, even though they can make money from farming and we are not allowed to farm."

"But how long will the savings last us, Bzalel?" Mama whispered back. "The fighting goes on and on."

Papa only sighed.

Since I was a little girl, I had known that there was a war going on in the world. But all I understood was that the Germans were fighting and killing the Russians. Then I had begun to hear my parents whispering about something called the Revolution. It meant nothing to me at all, except that first the Czar wasn't the Czar anymore, and then he and the Czarina and their children were dead. The children's deaths worried me especially.

"Papa, did the Czar's children know they were going to die? Would a czar's children have to be especially brave?" I asked.

But Papa had less energy to answer questions these days. He was very tired because he had to pull the wagon himself now. I still couldn't believe it, but Papa had sold Soos. Mama had cried when she saw Papa coming home one night without the big horse. He had sold the heavy wagon, too, and was using a kind of harness to pull a smaller cart, with all of his old goods piled high. Papa made light of the change, saying he'd received a good offer for Soos and the wagon and couldn't turn it down. He even pawed at the ground and neighed to make Nechama and me laugh. But when he slipped the harness off his shoulders, I heard him groan softly.

The worst part was that every night when he trudged home, his wagon was still filled with the same goods. "Very little sold today," he would say to Mama as he sank down in front of the stove. "The peasants don't have money to buy things anymore."

Mama didn't answer, but she took off his boots and brought warm water in a basin for his cold feet. One evening he reached up and pulled her against him, burying his face in her skirts. "There was typhoid in two villages," I heard him mutter.

I saw Mama shudder and slip her hand over Papa's cheeks and forehead. "A fever," I thought. "Was she feeling for a fever? Typhoid must be a sickness." Something else to worry about.

Like Papa, Mama, too, worked harder. She washed all our clothes herself in the big barrel in the kitchen, rather than paying Panya Truda to do it once a week. She bargained more firmly in the marketplace, but I could see that the peasants bargained just as desperately in return. Everyone was worried and there was little conversation between the Jews and the peasants. At least I didn't have to endure the taunts of the children on the other side of the pond: there was no more cholent to keep warm at Panya Truda's house.

I did feel scared, though, of the occasional loose bands of soldiers passing through our town. They were usually on foot and wore odd scraps of uniform. Some spoke Russian, others Polish. I was scared by their unshaven grim faces.

"Who are these soldiers, Papa?" I ventured.

"Soldiers?" he said in disgust. "Those are just thugs, bandits stealing food from poor people like us."

"Papa," I began, and then I stopped. The thing I was about to do was a hard sacrifice. I'd had the idea for days, and for days I'd been pushing myself closer and closer to doing it. It took some force—talking and talking and even a little shaking—until I finally persuaded Nechama to go along.

Papa looked at me inquiringly, and then he sat down and took me on his knee just as he used to in the old days. "What is it?" he prompted.

I had to swallow a painful lump in my throat. "Papa, you can sell our dolls for food. Nechama and I don't mind."

Papa grabbed me in a tight hug and I squeezed him back, blinking away the tears in my eyes.

Papa blew his nose. "Devorahleh." He smiled at me, stroking the hair back from my face. "You and Nechama are fine girls and we appreciate that you would give up your dolls for the family. Always take care of the family, my big girl. But you can keep your dolls."

"We can?" Nechama squeaked from behind the door where she had been eavesdropping.

I glared at the door.

"Yes." Papa laughed. "Enjoy them and play with them, because the peasants have no money for dolls now. Even potatoes are more precious today."

Papa pulled the cart alone for about half a year. I felt a little sick each morning to see him dragging it onto the rutted dirt tracks, turning to wave goodbye after adjusting the thick leather harness over his shoulders. Three kisses he would blow, the first one for Mama, of course, and then one each for Nechama and me, before pulling his cap down and making his way up the slight hill. The cart creaked and swayed behind him. It was lucky, I told myself, that Papa conquered the upward slope in the morning when he was fresh, while he descended the hill in the evening.

But one chilly fall morning when I was ten and Nechama seven, Papa couldn't pull the cart uphill. He couldn't even get up. I heard Mama lighting the fire to boil water while it was still dark. Then she bent over me. "Papa is sick," she whispered in a shaky voice. "I'm going to ask the barber for some medicine."

My stomach tightened. I slipped out of bed and ran over to stroke Papa's forehead. He smiled faintly at me, but he didn't look like my papa.

Mama returned alone, carrying a bottle carefully wrapped in some rags. Her face was pale and drawn.

"Go outside," she told us. "Go outside to the well and wash your faces." She began to lift the covers off Papa.

I left the room unwillingly, pushing Nechama in front of me. At the door I turned back for a moment. Mama and Papa were both looking anxiously at Papa's stomach, which seemed swollen and strange.

I turned the handle of the well to pump up a bucket of water. It felt icy, but I washed Nechama's hands and face and my own until they were red and shiny. Dear God, I prayed silently as I scrubbed, I'll be very good and I'll make Nechama be very good, and we'll do exactly as Mama tells us, if you'll only make Papa better.

The next day, Papa's face was grayer and he slept a lot. Neighbors and friends came to visit, whispering rather than talking. Papa didn't seem aware of any of them. I held his hand and wiped his face with care, but mainly his eyes were closed.

On the third morning, I woke from a cold, huddled sleep. Mama was crying, little peeping cries like a bird. I sprang out of bed to Mama's side and held her tight. Papa looked as if he was sleeping and there were no lines of pain or hunger around his eyes and mouth. But Mama's face was scrunched up and wet.

"He's gone, Devorahleh, Papa is gone," she whispered.

The world stopped. "No, no, no," I protested into Mama's shoulder. It could not possibly be that Papa was . . . dead.

Nechama squeezed into Mama's arms, too, her eyes confused as she turned from Mama to me and back again. She kept her face averted from Papa.

Mama held us both for a long time. A weight of cold and grayness pressed down on us. Then Mama put Nechama on my lap. She tucked the bedcover close around Papa, his shoulders, his legs, his feet. Then she slipped in next to him and pulled the cover around both of them. I think she was trying to keep the last bit of warmth in her bed.

# GOODBYE TO EASTERN EUROPE
## 1921

Isaac Ochberg's children were supposed to remain in Warsaw only a few weeks, just long enough to gather the two hundred who had been chosen. But as the last orphans arrived, the unthinkable happened.

I heard the news from Nechama, who came flying back to our cot in the old schoolhouse one morning, wailing loudly. "Daddy is sick, Daddy's sick," she said, sobbing. "Maybe he's going to die."

I stared at my sister. "Nechama! Papa's dead already! He died of the swelling," I cried, shaking her to bring her to her senses.

But Nechama kept crying and suddenly I realized what she meant. What will happen to us if Mr. Ochberg dies? I thought. My stomach froze into a ball of ice. What will we do, stranded here in a strange city? We wouldn't have left the orphanage if it wasn't for him. He's our leader.

I cast about in my mind for alternatives. If we were still

at the orphanage, we would be closer to our village. We could try to get home by cart. But there wasn't any home. Panya Truda had warned us that it wasn't safe to go back. So now we were stuck. Even Mr. Bobrow couldn't help. He wasn't South African; how could he take all of us to the safe country we were promised? Please, God, I prayed, please don't let Daddy Ochberg die.

I had told myself he was Mr. Ochberg. I had scorned the children who called him Daddy Ochberg, worshipped him, and wanted to walk next to him, sit next to him, hold his hand. But he was a good man, a kind man. And he took care of me.

That night and for nights afterward, Nechama and I joined the other orphans huddled outside the sickroom and we cried and prayed together. Some of the older boys knew Hebrew prayers; the others simply whispered to God in Yiddish. We understood one another. I felt close to the group for the first time.

After breakfast each day, Mr. Bobrow would try to call us to attention. "Come now, children, we must keep going with our lessons." But all of the faces matched my own feelings; we were too worried to concentrate on learning.

In the afternoons, I sat sipping my soup silently in Madame Engel's kitchen. Madame talked to her chief cook about Isaac Ochberg, and I grasped at every word for information.

"It's the influenza, Batya," Madame announced sadly. "The doctor says it's not the worst case he's seen, but it is that wicked flu."

"Tsk, tsk." Batya clicked her tongue as she stirred with her scarred wooden spoon. "My cousin who works at the central telegraph office says millions of people have died from it already. Even more than in the war."

My spoon felt like lead; I let it fall into my soup. Millions? But Daddy Ochberg couldn't die, he couldn't!

"I'm not surprised he came down sick," Madame said grimly. "That man is exhausted. Three months of traveling across Poland, Galicia, the Ukraine to gather his orphans, with most of the trains not working and gangs of bandits roaming the countryside."

"To think of the poor mites he had to leave behind . . . How on earth did he choose which children to save?" Batya asked curiously, wiping perspiration from her forehead with her ample linen apron.

"It nearly killed him to choose the lucky few," Madame said more quietly, her voice sad.

I blinked. I had nearly turned down Mr. Ochberg's invitation; I had gone with him only because Nechama insisted.

"The matron or principal of each orphanage helped him," Madame related. "He told me they used three conditions to choose. The children had to be full orphans: no mother, no father. They had to be healthy: he'd promised the South African government he wouldn't bring in any sick immigrants. And they had to really want to go with him."

After a pause, Batya asked, "Who's nursing Mr. Ochberg?"

"The oldest orphan, Laya," Madame told her. "The girl with braids who manages the small children's table at the restaurant. She's seventeen."

"That slip of a girl! How can she keep going day and night?" the cook asked with admiration in her voice.

"She's chosen two of the other teenagers to help her. You should have heard all the older children begging her to choose them, the angels," Madame answered. "They take turns at night, two of them sleeping for a few hours while the other watches him."

I bent forward over my soup to hide the tears in my eyes. I had wanted desperately to be one of the nurses. I knew I could do it. I remembered how I had helped Aunt Friedka to nurse Mama.

Then one night, Isaac Ochberg's fever began to drop. I was waiting outside the sickroom with Jente's solemn older sister, Liebe, early the next morning when Laya opened the door. A smile crept across her tired face.

"Good morning, Liebe; good morning, Devorah. The doctor said he thinks we are over the worst. Now, be quiet— no noise even if you're excited."

We raced off to wake the others with the news. This time it was my turn to run to my sister's bed.

"Nechama, he's getting better. Daddy's getting better!"

I heard what my own voice had said and I blushed. Daddy was getting better, but Papa had not gotten better;

Papa had died. Was it all right to be so glad now?

Nechama reached up to hug me tightly and then we hugged little Faygele and everyone else nearby. I can feel their hearts, I thought, I can feel each one's heart.

"Breakfast, and then your English class," called Mr. Bobrow. "We need to prepare ourselves for our new country." There was relief in his voice and his fingers trembled a little as he pushed up his spectacles.

Nechama couldn't stop talking about Africa. She heard from the bigger girls that there were diamonds in the mines, and gold. Why, if we just dug a little, we would be able to buy as many dolls as we wanted. And great bowls of milk, and even fruit.

Sometimes I, too, thrilled with excitement at the thought of a new life, but there was a sadness that I hadn't expected. It was the parting from Madame Engel. How could I leave my kind friend, who moved around her kitchen kingdom with her tall, regal bearing?

Daddy Ochberg is too busy to love any of the children more than the others, I thought. I never feel sure whether the special smile he gives me is given to each of the other children, too. But Madame's smile is just for me. Madame Engel is the only grownup person in the world now who cares about me the most. Mama and Papa died; Aunt Friedka was killed; but Madame is still here. How can I leave her?

Yet I hadn't been invited to stay. And there was

Nechama. Certainly Nechama would not change her mind about going to South Africa.

On our final morning in Warsaw, the sun outlined the gracious old buildings in gold as if to accentuate what we were leaving behind. We walked almost silently, two by two in a long line, to a dock on the banks of the Vistula River. Daddy Ochberg had almost all of his old energy as he packed us into a heavily laden riverboat.

"Pesha, you're in charge of the ten-to-twelve-year-olds," he called out. "Itzik, you take the eight-to-tens. Laya, you're good with the six-to-eights, and I'll manage the little ones with Mr. Bobrow. Children, put your suitcases under your benches and sit down. No moving around now."

I gulped as I saw Madame Engel arrive at the dock to say goodbye. Madame must have been up since dawn to pack the two hundred food bags she was handing out. My heart was tight with pain as I watched the familiar figure move slowly along the lines of children. Finally she reached me, stopped, and held out her arms. I flew into them.

"Thank you, thank you," I said, sobbing, but the words were strangled. I tightened my grip around her neck and buried my head under her chin.

Madame squeezed me close for a long time and then she held my face between her hands and looked into my eyes. Her face was as wet as mine. "You are strong as well as sad, mamaleh," she whispered. "Hold on to the strength, but let go of the sadness. It is up to you to make a new life now."

I stared at her. It was true; there was something inside me, something that Madame called strength, which held me up when I could not afford to fall. I nodded slowly.

"I am proud of you," she whispered.

The boat blew an echoing hoot, and Madame hugged me closer and kissed my forehead for a long time. I forgot my strength, cried out, and clutched her skirts. But she loosened my hands gently and kissed me one more time. Then she turned away slowly and walked up the ramp onto the shore.

The boat began to move. The other children chattered excitedly and blew goodbye kisses to Warsaw. I was alone. Madame Engel stood erect on the dock and waved farewell, her dark eyes looking directly at mine.

"Mama!" I called. The name forced itself out of me. "Mama!"

# THERE WAS NO ANGEL
## 1919–20

Although Mama climbed into Papa's deathbed and pulled the covers tight, there was no more warmth to be found. I don't remember the sun coming out once after that. Every day was cool, and I felt as if I were pushing through thick mist. Mama couldn't push. She never stood up straight again, it seemed to me. She didn't even prepare food for meals. Aunt Friedka moved into our house and took care of all of us.

Neighbors and friends came to visit each day for shiva, the traditional week of mourning. "We wish you long life," they murmured. "Long life, wish you long life."

Mama didn't seem to hear. She sat in a low chair or on the floor. The visitors' little children played outside with Nechama. Gradually the children's chatter and laughter began to penetrate the dim house.

"Nechama! Shhhh!" I ordered furiously from the front doorstep. "Be quiet! How can you play when Papa is dead?"

There was silence for a moment, and then Nechama burst into loud tears. I felt torn. I was glad that Nechama realized she had done wrong, but I hated to see the little face twisted in sobs. Hurrying to my sister, I hugged and kissed her and dried her face with my apron. Then I settled the small children under an old cherry tree and told them all to play very quietly.

But when I went back inside, Mama was staring downward and didn't seem to be aware of the commotion. A neighbor began to apologize for her children's part in the games, but Aunt Friedka cut her short. "They're still young," she said. "It would be better for Devorah to be out there with them."

How could she say such a thing? Of course it would be nice to run with the girls again, to be chased by the boys and shriek with laughter, but the time for such childishness was over. I sat down low next to Mama.

Exactly seven days after Papa was buried, visitors stopped coming. And so did the little gifts of food they had brought—two potatoes from one neighbor, a few strawberries and a bowl of milk from another. Aunt Friedka went out to barter for food every morning. She gave Nechama and me the biggest portions, but we felt hungry all the time. So did Aunt Friedka. Only Mama never complained.

Life went on somehow for a few months. Then came news of a pogrom in a Jewish shtetl to the west. Aunt Friedka whispered about it to our neighbors when she thought I wasn't listening. "I heard some Cossacks rode in and got all the Poles from the surrounding villages filled up with liquor. Strange bedfellows, Cossacks and Poles, but they get on well when it comes to killing Jews. Aagh, may the typhoid find its way to them!"

But the typhoid took a wrong turn. Mama woke up one morning burning with fever.

"Water," she cried. "My lips are parched, bring me water."

Aunt Friedka sprang up and examined Mama. I rushed to her, too. I could see small pink spots covering Mama's thin back and chest.

"Water, Devorah. Quickly!" Aunt Friedka ordered.

I sped to the well and pumped as fast as I could, then stumbled back with the bucket, water spilling over my bare feet.

"I'm coming, Mama. Water's coming," I said, panting. That was the first of many trips. Mama drank and drank, clutching the cup with shaking fingers, but the thirst couldn't be satisfied. Nechama was sent to a neighbor to keep her away from the fever, and Aunt Friedka tried to send me, too.

"No!" I declared. "I'm almost eleven; I'm old enough to look after my mama. I won't go."

"All right." Aunt Friedka gave up, turning back to Mama's bed. "I can use all the help I can get."

In the end she really did need me, because the barber said he could not come to help; he was busy.

"Busy!" Aunt Friedka exploded. "That lying coward.

Why doesn't he come straight out and say he's too scared to come near the typhoid."

Typhoid. It was the name of the terrible fever everyone feared. They said it could kill all the people in an entire village.

Aunt Friedka continued muttering. "Oh, he can take our money and treat us when we have the toothache or the gout, but when it's something he could catch, he's busy, is he? Devorah, build up the wood in that stove."

After that, Aunt Friedka and I had no time to talk. Mama wanted to drink water constantly; she needed her swollen dry lips moistened every few minutes and a cool damp cloth placed on the pounding pain in her forehead. Her feet were cold; then she was burning and sweating. Then her feet were cold again. The blankets had to be tucked in, removed, replaced. I thought my heart would snap the first time I saw my mama's legs. They were so thin, so bony and shrunken.

"But I can take care of her," I whispered to myself. "I want to take care of you, Mama."

Tears rolled hot and prickly as I ran to and from the well, but I didn't put down the bucket to wipe them away. I wanted every minute with Mama.

I had only two days. Some of the time Mama slept, but mostly she tossed and turned and moaned for water. She said lots of things that didn't make sense, and often she seemed to be speaking to her own mama, my grandmother, who was dead. On the second evening, Mama grew quiet, and when I moistened her lips, she gave a weak smile and whispered something very faintly.

"What, Mama?" I asked, bending forward to listen.

The words were soft as a cat's breath. "You're a good girl, Devorahleh. Take care of Nechama. Say your prayers every night. Never forget who we are."

I clung to her hand. "I'll never forget, Mama. I promise," I said, sobbing.

Then Mama whispered, "I'm going to Papa now. You stay with Nechama."

"Don't go, Mama!" I cried. "Mama! Mama! Don't leave us."

Mama's eyes closed and her breathing became rough. I felt Aunt Friedka's arms lifting me away, and I sobbed into her chest. There was a rattling sound from the bed. I turned back quickly, terrified of seeing the Angel of Death himself lifting my mother into the air. There was no angel. But my mama was dead.

# London Dream
## 1921

From Warsaw, the boat traveled down the Vistula River. I sat silently, staring at the riverbank. I glimpsed a tall woman pumping water vigorously at a well, and for a moment the woman was Aunt Friedka. I saw a man in a cart pulled by a horse. Papa? But the boat kept moving onward, and soon we were accosted by the shouts and smells of the huge and busy port of Danzig.

"Stay close to me," Daddy Ochberg ordered. "This is no place to get lost. Children, hold hands tightly. Don't let go!"

Two men carrying a heavy crate swore violently as an unbroken line of two hundred orphans with linked hands scuttled across their path. Another dockworker bent double to duck under our arms and hurried ahead, trailing an odor of sweat and garlic. The scream of steel grinding against steel hurt my ears.

"This way, this way." Even Mr. Bobrow sounded nervous as he called to us. "Our boat is this way. Stay together."

My fingers were sore from linking with Nechama's so tightly. I had to keep looking down to avoid slipping in the garbage strewn on the wet dock. Isaac Ochberg was up ahead, talking to the captain of the small freighter he had chartered.

"On board!" he called out to us, relief in his voice. "Here's our boat. Everyone on board."

The next part of the journey took longer, but I can't remember anything about it. There was no place to be but on the flat deck, and we sat or lay under a makeshift canopy of canvas, wrapped in all the clothes we owned. I felt sunk in heavy clay. I dozed and woke up to check that Nechama was nearby, then dozed again.

When I finally woke, my eyes opened to behold a scene finer than any dream. A gracious and glorious city was spread before our boat: bridges and towers, bells in belfries. There was a beautiful domed building that brought pleasure to my eyes, as Papa used to say, and a tall pillar supporting a statue of someone grand and proud. Blue glints shone like jewels among the feathers of strutting pigeons; the sun turned old blocks of stone to silver. Scrambling to my feet, I ran to the railing around the deck and stared and stared, drinking in the beauty.

Someone put an arm around my shoulders. It was

Daddy Ochberg. "I see you like London," he whispered. "I love London, too, little one. We'll wait here until a liner is ready to leave for South Africa." Then he hurried on.

"London, London," I repeated, softly so that the dream wouldn't vanish. But it only grew richer.

"Is that the King's palace?" Nechama asked me with wide eyes when our buses pulled up in front of a huge building with flags snapping in the wind. There were towers on either side, with ivy coloring the walls and framing hundreds of windows.

"No . . ." I answered uncertainly. "I heard Mr. Bobrow say the Jewish people of London have paid for us to stay in a hotel."

A hotel. None of us had ever stayed in a hotel before. As we climbed down from the bus, a hush fell. The hotel had the strangest entrance I had ever seen. Framed in brass was a huge glass door that moved around in a circle. People were walking through it casually and disappearing. Then other people would appear in their place, walking around the circle in the opposite direction.

"Follow me," urged Daddy Ochberg, and only because he was Daddy was I brave enough to shuffle through that door. "And out you step, quickly now," Daddy warned as the door spun Nechama and me into the hotel lobby.

I had never dreamed of such a place, glittering with chandeliers and polished brass. The lobby was much bigger and even more beautiful than Madame Engel's restaurant. Out of the corner of my eye, I saw Nechama crouch down.

"Ooh, soft," she was murmuring, stroking the thick red and gold carpeting.

"Nechama, stand up. You're embarrassing me," I told her.

There wasn't time to linger in the lobby. A boy wearing a shiny uniform and a cap with a gold ribbon led us to a tiny mirrored room where a lady in a different uniform and white gloves stood next to a panel of buttons on the wall. As more and more children were squeezed into the small space, I hung back. But then Nechama stepped in without hesitation, so I had to follow. Suddenly the lady pulled a lever, the gold-barred door clanged shut, and the entire mirrored room began to shudder upward. My eyes opened wide with alarm. Nechama let out a cry. The boy in the uniform lifted his gloved hand too late to cover his grin; then the doors opened again and he led us out.

Somehow we had been transported to a completely different place, a long hallway lined with doors. The boy stopped at one of the doors, opened it with a big brass key, and pointed us into a room. It was almost completely filled with small beds. Immediately, Nechama scrambled onto one of the strange firm mattresses and began to jump up and down.

"Whee!" she shouted. "Try it, Devorah. There is some kind of bouncy straw inside here!"

I knew I should stop Nechama from bouncing on the bed, but I was too busy staring at the flowered curtains and the pretty pictures on the walls. This was where we were to sleep?

Even better was to come. The boy gestured us to follow him, and he led us down the hall and pushed open the door to a big room. I peeked inside. Everything was white: white floors, white walls, and a gleaming white tub the size of a horse trough, standing on curvy white legs.

Nechama ran straight in and fingered with interest some little brass wheels at the end of the bath. I hurried in after her to stop her from touching the strange things.

"Aha!" said the boy with another grin, his face lighting up with understanding. "*On*, turn it *on*," he commanded, showing me to turn one of the wheels to the left.

*Whoosh!* Water rushed out of a gold-colored pipe and thundered into the bath. I jumped back. The boy doubled over in good-natured laughter. I stared at the indoor waterfall, and then I also burst out laughing.

"See here?" The boy pointed. "Hot. Very hot." He pretended to burn his hand. "And this one is cold. Very cold." He shivered dramatically.

My eyes shone. No more heavy pumps, no more icy splashing in the morning. I wished Papa and Mama could see the magical bathroom.

But a short time later, when we sat down to eat, I couldn't bear to think about Papa and Mama. They would have fattened up handsomely, they would never have become sick and died if they had had even a fraction of this meal. Milk, hot tea, cheese, apples, slices of soft white bread stuck together with butter and jam, even cake with slivers of nuts and bits of fruit in it. I ate until my stomach stuck out like a ball.

The next morning I woke to angel music: all the bells of London were chiming, leading and following in charmingly uncoordinated peals. "Nechama, wake up! Listen!" I whispered, and Nechama opened sleepy eyes and smiled back at me. "Let's get dressed quickly," I urged. What would the new day bring in this wonderful place?

After breakfast, Daddy Ochberg announced, "We will all gather in the writing room now. We have had donations of clothing, and they will be given out according to your sizes."

But the best was hidden at the bottom of a sturdy steamer trunk of dresses. Daddy Ochberg reached in deep and lifted out a pile of big colored boards with bright pictures on them. He opened the top one, revealing many pages.

"A book!" I exclaimed.

Daddy Ochberg turned to me with a smile. "Are you more interested in books than in pretty dresses, mamaleh?" he asked.

"Mama used to let me dust Papa's books sometimes," I said softly. "There were only a few, but they smelled good, of leather, and the pages were so thin and soft." I stretched out my hand and dared to touch. "I've never seen books like these, though, with colors and pictures."

"And I've never heard you say so many words in a row." Daddy Ochberg smiled. "How would you like to be our librarian?"

I didn't know what a librarian was, but it had to have something to do with those books, so I nodded my head vigorously.

"Come and stand next to me," Daddy Ochberg said.

I stumbled past the other children, my cheeks flaming at the whispers and stares.

"Devorah Lehrman," he announced in a formal voice, "is now our librarian, and all books given to us will be kept under her bed. When any of you wants to read a book, you may go to her and ask to choose one. Then you must sign your name on a piece of paper and you can keep the book for three nights. That is what we call a library."

"Devorah's only twelve," objected Itzik. "Why is she the lyberian?"

"Because she loves books and she is responsible," replied Daddy Ochberg firmly, putting an arm around my shoulders. "I know she'll take care of things."

My face was on fire and my hands were sweating. "I can carry them all to my room myself," I said, and I didn't stop to rest until I reached my door, even though my fingers were numb with the weight. Kneeling on the floor, I sorted out the books on my bed. Those with many pictures and only a few big words were obviously for the little children; those with tiny, difficult English writing and only one single picture at the beginning, with a thin sheet of tissue to protect it, must be for Laya and Pesha's age group.

As for myself, I was determined to look through them

all. I started immediately with the easiest ones, poring over the shiny pages bearing mysterious pictures, such as a boy flying through the air, a rabbit dressed in a blue jacket, and a baby boy living in a den of wild animals.

Nechama didn't return to our room until almost dinnertime; she had been trying on new dresses and coats with her friends in their room. She twirled around a few times to show me her finery, brushed down her curls, and left again. But a few other children came in timidly, and I helped each of them to choose a book and write down their names. I even tried to read a story to little Malke, making up the words I couldn't understand by looking at the pictures.

Suddenly a very loud bang made Malke flinch next to me. I hugged her in fright. Then I laughed. "It's just the door, Malke! The wind blew it open against the closet." The door swung closed again, and as it did I caught a glimpse of myself in the mirror on the back. Myself? Was that me? There was a girl sitting on a soft bed, holding a colorful book in her hand. She had long wavy hair falling around her face, and she wore a relieved smile, which made her look quite pretty. I blushed and hugged Malke again.

When I was with the books, I was safe. And not only safe, I was rich and royal, brave and beautiful. Papa's stories rested at the bottom of my memory while I found new legends, with pictures of creatures that Mr. Bobrow told me were called dragons and ogres and fairy godmothers. The monstrous Cossacks and devouring fires of my nightmares were replaced during the day by muscled gladiators in leather tunics and the volcanic lava that covered Pompeii hundreds of years before. I lay on my stomach, my thick braid clenched between my teeth, escaping into the pages.

But my shyness returned when we were visited by kind London matriarchs and even entire families with elaborately dressed children who stared at us curiously. It was Nechama, fearless and smiling angelically, who was often chosen to greet the visitors with her best English sentence: "Gut-day, my naam is Nechama." One little visitor was holding a doll in exquisite lace clothing, and Nechama kept staring at it. Afterward she announced firmly, "I'm going to have a doll like that in South Africa."

I didn't say a word, but I promised myself that somehow I would replace the doll Nechama had lost on the Night of the Burning.

One morning, Daddy Ochberg woke us early. He seemed flustered. "Up you get, rise and shine, get yourselves washed and dressed. And see that you clean behind your ears, too, and comb your hair perfectly. We are going to have special, very special, visitors."

Off he hurried. Within minutes, the rumor jumped from room to room: the King and Queen of England were coming to see the two hundred orphans who were on their way to South Africa. The King and Queen of England were actually coming to visit us.

Nechama squealed and jumped up onto her bed to dance a little jig, but my own excitement made me shivery and quiet. I was going to see a real live king and queen, just like the ones in the storybooks.

At breakfast I couldn't eat, not even my favorite white toast and scrambled eggs. Afterward we were led to the hotel lobby and organized into a tight group.

"Let's practice the English anthem one more time!" Mr. Bobrow ordered. "Sing with all your might now, children. Remember, since you will be citizens of the Union of South Africa, the English king is your king. Let me hear—"

At that moment Daddy Ochberg hurried in from his lookout position outside the revolving doors. I had never seen him dressed so smartly, or looking so nervous.

"The King and Queen are coming. Stand at attention and make me proud of you all," he announced.

He rushed outside again, straightening his cravat, and a long moment later the hotel manager and Daddy Ochberg led in a bearded man and a serious-looking woman in street clothes, followed by a group of more men and women. I kept my eyes on the revolving doors, determined to see the golden King and Queen at the exact moment of their majestic arrival.

But Daddy Ochberg was lifting his arms in a signal to begin. The other children burst enthusiastically into a rendition of the anthem. "God save our gracious King," they trumpeted, and the man and woman smiled very slightly.

The woman wore a soft cream-colored dress and a hat with a little veil over her face. The man had a close-cropped beard like that of the late Czar. It was not until the woman gracefully accepted a bouquet of flowers from giggling little Faygele that I was forced to admit the truth. These kind but ordinary people, without even a hint of a tiara or a rich purple cape, were the King and Queen of England.

"I'm tired," I whispered to Mr. Bobrow after the couple had been ushered out by the hotel manager, who walked bent at the waist in an ingratiating bow. "May I go to my room, please?"

As soon as I was alone, I threw myself on my bed and sobbed bitterly. I had been so excited to see royalty, and they had seemed so ordinary. Why, on High Holidays back home, the butcher's wife wore fancier dresses than this Queen of England. I blew my nose and reached under the bed for a book about a real king with an ermine cape and a bejeweled crown. Now, that was a king before whom I'd be honored to sing.

A few nights later, on my way to the big white bathroom, I passed the hotel room that served as an office and headquarters for Daddy Ochberg and Mr. Bobrow. Hearing their voices inside, I pressed my ear against the door and eavesdropped.

They were talking about arrangements a certain ship

was making to have kosher food aboard for us. Then Daddy Ochberg gave a big sigh of relief. "Two more days and we will be on our way home. I will only rest easy when I deposit the children at the orphanage."

I slipped back into my bed and lay shivering even though it wasn't cold. It was time to say yet another goodbye—to this magical city. I wanted to stay in London, but not because it would ever feel like home. No, I was scared, very, very scared of the strange land we were venturing to, even farther from my village.

"Domachevo. Domachevo," I whispered again and again until I fell asleep. But instead of dreaming of the warm stove in our home, the familiar muddy lanes, the pine forests along the Bug River, I dreamed of wild flames leaping. Aunty Friedka's limp body. Wet knives. The Night of the Burning.

# THE NIGHT OF THE BURNING
## August 1920

At night, Aunt Friedka sat in Papa's chair next to the stove, mending Nechama's stockings or making a skirt for me out of Mama's old apron.

Orphans, I thought bleakly. Since Mama went to be with Papa, Nechama and I are orphans. What a horrible word. I moved a little closer to Aunt Friedka. But we're with Aunty, in our own house. Aunty is our . . . rock. Aunt Friedka's lips were pursed tightly and her eyes were unreadable, her face as closed as it had been since they had finally brought Uncle Pinchas home from the army.

In the six months that had passed since Mama died, Nechama had been unable to sleep without both Aunt Friedka and me holding her, so we all slept together in Mama and Papa's old bed. One night we were beginning to prepare for bed when Aunt Friedka said, "Shh!"

We were startled by her sharp tone. Then I heard it, too. Far away, people were crying out and there was the sound of thunder. No, it wasn't thunder, it was horses' hooves. Men were shouting and women were screaming.

With a crash, the door flew open and a voice yelled through the opening, "Pogrom! Hide! Run away! Pogrom!" And the voice was gone.

Aunt Friedka was on her feet in a bound, like a mother lion. "Food? Money? No, just go." With one shove she pushed us through the open door, rushed out herself, and slammed the front door behind us.

My mind was racing, jumping. I had my family photograph safe with me; I carried that always in my pocket. "The candlesticks, Aunty!" I shouted. "We must save Mama's brass candlesticks."

Nechama joined in with a wail. "My doll!"

"There's no time. Save our lives!" my aunt shouted back. Her face was open again and I read it clearly: Aunt Friedka was frightened, terrified. My stomach dropped so fast I almost vomited.

Aunt Friedka was barricading the house with crazy haste, blocking the door with a huge wooden bar that was usually stored just under the eaves and locking it with a key that hung on a chain she always wore. I'd never thought to ask what the key was for. She grabbed Nechama with one hand and clutched my wrist with the other, a cold fierce grip that felt like iron. Then we ran, away from our home.

"Where to?" I gasped as my legs pumped.

"Away from the noise. To the shul."

Ahead, in the light of the full moon, I saw whiteness

everywhere.

Am I going mad? I thought. I see snow but it's not falling from the sky. It's not snow, it's . . . Floating through the air and piling up in drifts were thousands and thousands of feathers. I turned my head to stare as Aunt Friedka pulled us along. Feather beds and feather pillows lay slumped on the ground. They had been sliced open and tossed out of the windows of Jews' homes. Broken chairs and splintered tables had been smashed by axes or hurled onto the rutted path.

"Oh God, oh God," Aunt Friedka whispered, and Nechama whimpered. There was no one in sight, and only the sound of screaming from somewhere behind us.

Then we heard a roar in front of us, and Aunt Friedka suddenly changed direction. She pulled us off the road and down a muddy alley and half fell, half knelt behind a wooden fence. It was the same cracked fence where Nechama and I would hide with our girlfriends while we waited for the boys to come out of school.

We peered between the planks and my eyes widened. Twenty, maybe thirty peasants swarmed in and out of the synagogue, their excited faces lit by the flaming torches they held high. One of them carried an open bottle of vodka and many were unsteady on their feet. They were looting the synagogue with loud determination. Some dumped piles of worn prayer books into the mud. Several gleefully rattled the silver bells and silver chains and engraved shields used to decorate the Torah scrolls.

When one drunken man ran past, clutching under his arm a velvet Torah cloth with its rich golden embroidery, I stuffed my whole hand into my mouth to keep from gasping. He was one of the farmers whose stall my mother used to visit in the market. Two peasants laughed triumphantly as they danced out of our synagogue brandishing the precious parchment scrolls between them. The scrolls that we treated with such loving care. The tiny black letters that our Torah reader followed respectfully with a carved silver pointer rather than touching them with his own finger. The two men cavorted and stumbled, and the parchment ripped with a sickening sound.

Then I saw the rabbi. He stood silently outside the synagogue, beside a villager who kept one big hand on the rabbi's long white beard and the other hand around a thick wooden club. The rabbi's yarmulke had been knocked off and his black coat was covered in mud. His eyes were closed; his lips moved in silent prayer. I saw him only for a moment before I closed my own eyes. But I couldn't close my ears.

"Where's the money? Where did you hide your Jewish money?" someone shouted at the rabbi.

"Moneylending bloodsuckers!" someone else yelled.

Then the first voice shouted again, "This is for killing our Lord Jesus Christ!" There was the sound of a blow and a dull grunt.

My aunt pulled us up and away. I didn't ask where we were running to this time. If the synagogue was not safe, where could we possibly go?

As we stumbled along, a strong smell of smoke filled my nose and I heard crackling.

"They're burning the houses," a woman called out as she ran past. Aunt Friedka hesitated, then followed her. On the edge of the village, standing alone, was the large barn owned by the dairyman. The woman ran up to the big wooden door and disappeared inside. Aunt Friedka led us after her into the blackness.

Nechama and I had gone into the barn many times to buy milk since we sold our goat. The familiar smells surrounded us. The cows were all inside, their halters making a clinking sound as they shifted uneasily.

Feeling her way across the hay scattered on the floor, my aunt pulled us to the very back. Then we all scrambled up the ladder into the loft. The woman and her family were also hiding there, and we looked at one another in shock. I knew the children from Shabbes mornings at the synagogue, but we didn't exchange a word. Everything was upside down; everything was awful.

"We can see the whole village from here," Aunt Friedka said, hurrying over to the open window.

I followed her. It didn't look like our village. The sky was a strange color from the smoke and the fiery light. Houses flamed like giant torches, their insides black and their outsides an angry red. Dark figures crossed and recrossed in front of the fires, moving quickly, carrying things, throwing things.

The biggest fire was in the tallest building, a beautiful tall building, a building of beauty. The synagogue was burning.

"We're going to be trapped up here," came a sob from the woman we had followed. "They'll burn the barn. Out, children. We'll run down to the river."

The other family half climbed, half fell down the ladder and were gone. I started to follow them, but Aunt Friedka's hand caught my shoulder. "Better to risk burning than to be out there in the night where they will beat and stab us to death for sure," she said.

Nechama burst into loud tears. A violent shudder went through my body. How can this be true? Oh, Mama, Papa, please make this just a very bad dream.

I turned back to the window. "Aunt, look!" I cried, pointing down at the cobblestone road that led away from the village square right past the barn.

Screaming and running in sheer terror, falling and getting up to run again, was a crowd of Jews, old people, children, women clutching babies, my neighbors and my friends. Soldiers riding high up on huge snorting horses were chasing them, herding them like animals. They wore uniforms I'd never seen before, with high shiny boots, and carried long whips. Their faces were terrible with excitement and I could hear their hoarse shouts—they were Russians.

"Cossacks," Aunt Friedka spat out. "So that's who gave the villagers their chance to turn on us."

Suddenly a number of Jews broke away from the

screaming crowd and rushed toward the barn. Several Cossacks chased them, jumping off their moving horses, landing skillfully on their feet, and running into the barn.

"Please no, not in here," Aunt Friedka cried. She rushed over to the ladder to look down and I was right behind her. Nechama wept into my back, but her voice was almost lost in the hideous screams below.

The Cossacks pulled out long knives. As if they were slaughtering cattle, they began to kill everyone in the barn. I saw. I saw people running, blinded by blood pouring from their heads, cut down from behind, and finally still. Men. Women. Children.

I didn't realize that Aunt Friedka was sobbing until the sobbing stopped and my aunt's breath caught loudly. A Cossack had noticed the ladder, was looking up at us, had one hand on the ladder, was climbing up with his knife raised.

I shrieked. Aunt Friedka moved quickly. As the Cossack's head reached the level of the loft, she lifted her skirt and kicked hard. I heard a grunt and for a moment the man swayed, his left hand clutching tightly to the wooden floor of the loft. He was so close I could smell vodka on his breath, could see his eyes clouded with rage. Then he took one step higher, lifted his right hand, and stabbed furiously, stabbed and stabbed and stabbed. Aunt Friedka gasped, pushed her hand against the sharp knife as if she could stop it, as if she could stop anything. And then she fell heavily on top of Nechama and me.

There was a curse and a thud. The Cossack must have lost his balance and dropped off the ladder to the barn floor. Nechama let out a high-pitched scream, but I was past screaming. I waited silently for the Cossack to climb back up again and finish his job. We were going to be killed. I waited.

Below, the screams had turned to a few faint moans. I heard a sudden sharp command, rapid footsteps, then the beat of horses galloping away from the barn. Silence.

After a few minutes, perhaps a long time, Aunt Friedka's body became unbearably heavy on top of me. I couldn't think; I refused to think. With all my strength, I managed to crawl out from under my aunt, and I pulled Nechama out, too. Then, dragging my sister, I crept away from the ladder. Just a little farther, Devorah, I told myself, just a little farther. If we can only get to that hay at the far end. No one stopped us. I crawled and dragged, crawled and dragged, then I curled around Nechama and pulled hay over both of us. There was dry hay dust in my mouth and wet blood all over my dress. Not my blood. Not Nechama's.

"Shh," I said to Nechama, without feeling anything at all. "Don't start screaming again or I'll cover your mouth to keep you quiet." Nechama turned wide, crazy eyes on me, but she gave only a few last desperate hiccuping sobs. I put my arms around my sister. I don't remember anything more after that.

Loud rustling in the straw woke me the next morning. I

was frozen from cold and shock and my arms were stiff from holding Nechama. I saw two large, unlaced boots approach across the loft, a woman's stockings rising above them. Slowly I lifted my head above the hay and looked up at a strangely familiar face. It was Panya Truda, the Christian villager who used to keep our cholent warm for Shabbes lunch and who had washed our clothes once a week when we had had money to pay her. Panya Truda's face was white and her hands were shaking as she reached down to touch Nechama's still body. Nechama stirred in her sleep and Panya Truda gasped.

"Stay still," she ordered me. "I will send my daughter to find someone to take you away."

Then she shut her eyes for a moment. "O Lord Jesus, help the babies, they are the only ones," she muttered.

I knew I should not think. I felt for the photograph in my pocket and kept touching it with my icy fingers. It seemed a long time before Panya Truda and her grown daughter came back with two blankets, which they wrapped around Nechama and me, completely covering our heads and eyes. They lifted us up like bundles, then carried us down the ladder and across the barn. Panya Truda sobbed softly as she stumbled over large objects on the ground.

Outside, there was a bitter smell of smoke. Burning torches in the night. I would not think. Nechama and I were put down onto something quite soft. I could tell from her quick breathing that she was awake and terrified.

Then Panya Truda drew the blankets down from our

heads, and I could see that we were lying in the back of a cart with a layer of hay on the bottom. Panya Truda was standing between us and the barn so that she blocked our view. She whispered urgently, "Devorah, Nechama, this man is taking his cart back to Pinsk. It is far away. He said he will take you with him, to some Jews there. I have put bread and cheese and milk for you right here in the cart. Do not come back. There is no one left here. May your god forgive us."

She spoke briefly to a stranger sitting at the front of the cart. He clucked to his horse and the cart began to move away from the village. Soon we rounded a curve and I could no longer see Panya Truda standing still in the center of the track. The driver was looking straight ahead as if he didn't want to know what he was carrying. I huddled down into the hay, pulled my little sister back into my arms, and tried to sleep again, stroking Nechama's head when she cried softly for Mama.

I don't know how many days we rode. Once, the driver drove the cart hurriedly off the road to make way for a band of rough-looking young Polish boys, and another time he had to wait while a large group of soldiers trudged past. "Reds," the driver called the soldiers as he spat at their backs from a distance. "Bloody Reds. May Jesus Christ save the souls of the sweet Czar and his family."

I kept silent. I hugged Nechama and fingered my photo of Papa and Mama, baby Nechama, and me as a little girl. We were all together in the photo.

# THE SHIP TO AFRICA
## September 1921

We departed London for South Africa on September 2, 1921. Each of us carried a knapsack with a change of English clothing, and some of us had a few belongings from home. In my coat pocket was the old photograph of my family.

The first time I saw our ship on the great Southampton dock, I came to a sudden halt. "Move on, you're blocking the way!" one of the children behind me called irritably. Then, as the others saw the white vision, they, too, froze.

"That's not what you would call a . . . boat," Itzik said slowly, while the other big boys around him whistled appreciatively. I murmured my agreement. The majestic ship rose several levels into the air, dazzlingly high and white, with the British flag right at the top. The deck was lined with blue railings that seemed to extend forever to the left and right of us. Below the deck were lines of funny windows, all perfectly round. There must be levels of rooms all the way down, maybe even some under the water. The ship was bigger than the hotel, bigger than the whole village of Domachevo.

"The *Edinburgh Castle!*" Mr. Ochberg announced. "She's the queen ship of the Union-Castle shipping line, children. A bit worn from her service during the war, but a treat for us all."

At the top of the gangplank, two sailors wearing lightning-white uniforms with sun-gold buttons were as polite to us as if we were adults.

"Welcome aboard," they said. "We hope you have a pleasant voyage." I drew myself up to look taller and more dignified, but Nechama was bouncing with excitement next to me. "Faygele said she heard there are two ballrooms and a big pond for swimming!" I looked at her in disbelief. How could a ship have a pond where you could swim? And why would a ship need two rooms for people to play with balls?

Soon I felt too sick to wonder about anything. I discovered that there were indeed several levels under the water, and our cabins were at the lowest level. Down there, the ship creaked loudly and frighteningly. There were no windows and no fresh air, and the smell of oil hung above the tightly wedged lines of bunks. We lay side by side and groaned. Soon the stench of vomit was added to the odor.

"I want to go home. I want to get off," Faygele moaned. "Stop the ship."

Each time I tried to get up to help, bile rose to my

throat and I fell back onto my bunk. In the bunk above me, Nechama escaped from sickness into a blind sleep. A kind Englishwoman who had volunteered to escort us to South Africa bustled in and out of our cabins, murmuring in her broken Yiddish. Braindel and Rosha, smug in their immunity to seasickness, helped her to bring buckets and wet facecloths and a little dry toast.

After that first long day, my stomach began to settle. I tried standing up, holding my belly with both hands. Nechama slept on. The Englishwoman had promised I'd feel better outdoors, so, clinging to the moist railing, I climbed slowly up the black iron stairs to the open deck. A cool salty breeze filled my lungs as a vast green dreamscape unrolled in front of me, bejeweled with white foam and swirling with ever-shifting designs. I fell instantly in love with the ocean.

After that I didn't go downstairs except to sleep. Hour after hour, the wind soothed my thoughts as I gazed at the water that seemed a world unto itself. Maybe the ocean is a mirror reflection of heaven, I thought dreamily. Maybe Mama and Papa are floating in a paradise of green and blue swells, weightless, sunlit.

I began saving bits of food from my meals for the seagulls, which soared effortlessly between heaven and ocean. If I held out a bit of bread and kept perfectly still, a white creature of the sky would skim down with strong wings and perch briefly on my wrist with dry, scratchy toes.

One day, I was so absorbed in the gulls that I was

caught off guard. Two sailors had been watching me, and before I knew it they had walked right up to me.

"Good morning," one said in Polish.

I dropped my bread and stared at them. My eyelid twitched. What were these men in uniform going to do to me?

"My name's Pete. Used to be Piotr when I was a kid in Poland. What's your name?" he continued with a friendly grin. The other sailor was smiling kindly, too.

"Devorah," I ventured.

"How do you like the *Edinburgh Castle*?" Pete asked. His Polish sounded stiff, as if he hadn't spoken it for a long time, and sometimes he inserted a few English words. It was the Polish of Panya Truda—and of the villagers who burned our shul.

I managed to give a nod, which apparently satisfied him.

"Beautiful, isn't she?" Pete agreed before turning to say a few words in English to his companion. "My friend Joe here wants you to try his peppermint toffees, so let's sit down for a bit and we'll tell you the story of the *Edinburgh Castle*."

Before I had a chance to wonder about danger, I was sucking on a candy that filled my mouth with a delicious icy fire, and Pete was telling me sea tales. It turned out that Joe spoke some German, which is similar to Yiddish, and also that he had a comic talent for acting out the meaning. When he imitated a greedy gull, I startled myself by sending a real laugh out into the wind, my head giddy with sea air and freedom.

Nechama and some playmates found me on the deck and gaped at my new friends.

"Where you sleep, there's not much fresh air, is there?" Pete said to Nechama and me and the rest of the growing audience. "Yessir, we can see it in your faces!"

Joe performed a little pantomime of the children rolling from side to side and then being sick into the ocean. Bubbly laughter opened my chest.

"Now come along with us, don't be shy," Pete continued. "We're going to show you the posh quarters for the toffs up above."

We followed Pete and Joe on the tour. It soon became clear that "posh" meant fancy and "toffs" meant wealthy people. After a quiet conversation with a sympathetic steward, Pete and Joe allowed us to peek into a spacious suite with real beds and a separate sitting area, oil paintings and gold light sconces on the walls, and immense bowls of flowers everywhere. We gasped in admiration.

"That's a stateroom," Pete explained proudly. "The King's first cousin once slept in that very bed."

"We sang for the King," piped up Nechama. "The Queen smiled at me."

It was the sailors' turn to be impressed. "Blimey," Joe said. "I'm honored to meet such famous singers." He swept a grand curtsy to the ground.

I laughed along with the rest. There was no need to

mention how disappointed I'd been in the King and Queen. "Blimey." That sounded like a useful word to remember.

·Many of the other third-class passengers were also friendly and spent hours teaching us songs and drawing funny pictures for us on scraps of paper. I tried drawing, too, and one of them admired my sketch of our village. "You have artistic talent," he said, in front of everyone.

The unexpected compliment made me bold enough to ask him and his Yiddish-speaking friends, "Did you know anyone from a village called Domachevo?" But most of the refugees wanted to talk about the future rather than the past.

One day, I noticed a group of smartly dressed men and women peering down at us from the deck for first-class passengers.

"I wish they'd stop staring," I whispered to Nechama, squirming uncomfortably.

"I don't mind. Some ladies in beautiful dresses came down and gave us sweets and little cakes this morning."

"Weren't you shy?" I asked.

"No, because the cakes had thick pink icing on them," replied Nechama.

I opened my mouth to remonstrate. How was I supposed to keep Nechama safe if she went around talking to strangers? Then I remembered my own quick friendship with the kind sailors, and I shut my mouth again.

Seventeen days after we left London, I was awakened by loud noises and shouted commands. I trembled. I was suddenly back with Nechama and Aunt Friedka as a neighbor shouted warnings of a pogrom.

But Nechama squealed happily in the bunk above me. "Pete was right. He said we'd reach Africa today." She pulled on a skirt and shirt and was gone.

"Wait, Nechama. Put on something warm," I ordered. Then I gave up, scrambling into my clothes and carrying Nechama's coat under my arm as I chased my sister up the flights of stairs to the main deck.

It was still early in the morning; the sun had not yet risen. But below the skies, in the distance, was land. A surprisingly large, mistily purple, mountainous land. South Africa. We could see South Africa.

"Look at the mountain that's completely flat at the top," Pete called out to us as he hurried past. "That one's called Table Mountain."

A pure white tablecloth of clouds hung down over the edges of the mountain. It reminded me of something. "The table's ready for Shabbes dinner," I whispered to myself. But Nechama overheard and turned to smile at me. We were remembering the same Shabbes table. My eyes blurred with tears.

By the time I could see clearly again, the ship had drawn closer to the great land mass, which glimmered with thousands of lights. The white sparkles were woven into diamond necklaces swinging from the breasts of the mountains down to the dark sea.

I gasped. "It looks like fairyland in my English books."

The sun came up slowly. All of us were on deck now, chattering and pointing. We could just make out small moving shapes on the dock.

"Those are people!" Nechama exclaimed. "Look at all the people waiting to meet us."

"There must be hundreds," I said.

"Thousands," Laya said with awe.

"Yes, the whole town's turned out to see what monkeys Daddy Ochberg has brought them!" Little Faygele giggled.

We laughed excitedly.

"They must really want us," Nechama said to me, and we squeezed hands.

The crowd on the wharf became clearer. There were adults and children, swaying together from side to side. And gradually the sound of singing crept over the water and reached our ship.

A thrill rippled through me. "Nechama," I said, "Papa taught us that song, remember?"

Nechama leaned over to listen and a faint recognition lit her eyes. "I think I remember. Sing it for us. What does it mean?" she asked.

I started to sing softly. In an instant, the children around me had picked up the words, or at least had remembered the beautiful melody, and we swayed arm in arm as we sang again and again:

"Hinei ma tov u'ma nayim
Shevet achim gam yachad.

How good and how pleasant it is
When families dwell together in unity."

The group on the dock could hear us singing, too, and their own singing became louder. Back and forth the words traveled. Voices rose and linked across the water in the dawn's light, a ribbon of sound threading us closer and closer, singing of safety and reunion.

# Home to the Orphanage
## 1921

From our bus, festooned with streamers by the welcoming crowd at the Cape Town dock, I saw a strange world. How very different it was from Europe. My part of Poland was flat and brown and marshy; even London had been gray most days. But Cape Town in spring was like a painting from one of my books. It was as if someone had decided to draw the bluest of blue skies and an emerald ocean and golden mountains between. Then the sun had been painted in, with a wash of color kissing everything.

The people, too, were of many different colors. The Jews who had greeted us so kindly had been almost as white as we were, and I saw other whites walking and driving on the streets. Many people were a glowing and very definite brown. Those in between in color seemed to talk in a lilting singsong. Then there were lightly colored women with long, straight, and brilliant black hair, wearing slim pants underneath bright tunics.

"What are those people eating?" Nechama asked me, pointing out the window at a white woman and her little girl sitting on a park bench and sharing what looked like a large, curved, pale yellow finger. As we stared, the woman casually pulled off a thick skin. I shivered, remembering the whispers about cannibals I had heard in the orphanage in Pinsk.

The bus made a sharp turn into the shadow of the mountains and puffed along a gravel driveway through a forest of pines. It stopped in front of a large, gracious building. At the door waited a smiling woman in a starched white uniform and a white nurse's cap. Hanging out of the windows of the orphanage were fifty, sixty, maybe seventy sturdy and tanned South African children, staring with unabashed curiosity. We stared back.

Daddy Ochberg stood up to greet the woman. "Lunch first, Matron, then playtime," he called as he stepped out. "These children have been cooped up in close quarters for too long."

We climbed down, nudging against Daddy Ochberg and one another like scared lambs. Nechama had lost all her breezy optimism about Africa. "Itzik said there will be spiders and snakes under our beds. Will there? I didn't like the thing that woman was eating in the park. Will there be real food here?" she whispered. I didn't have any answers.

After a few hours, we agreed that the food was as good as in London and that, although there were a few spiders, there didn't seem to be any snakes. Then Faygele burst out laughing. "This place is so crowded that there isn't any room for snakes!"

"The children are right," Mr. Bobrow told Daddy Ochberg and Matron. "Even after half of the children leave for Johannesburg tomorrow, where will we put the rest? Your new wing won't be ready for weeks."

Half of the children leaving for Johannesburg? I turned to Daddy Ochberg in shock. After all this time together?

Daddy Ochberg saw my face and reached down to smooth my hair back. "Everything will be all right, Devorah of the big dark eyes," he said. To Mr. Bobrow, he answered, smiling, "We will stretch the walls." And we did. All of us slept in two long rooms, some in small beds and others on close-packed mattresses on the floor. Little suitcases spilled their contents everywhere.

The next day, one hundred of Daddy's orphans were sent by train from Cape Town to the Jewish orphanage in Johannesburg. Nechama and Faygele sobbed as they waved goodbye to those who were leaving us. But my eyes were dry and the muscles in my face felt like stone. I wouldn't say another goodbye; I couldn't. I turned my face away as the bus rumbled down the driveway between the pines.

"Goodbye." "Bye." "Write to us soon." "Goodbye." When the shouts of farewell had curled up toward the mountains and disappeared in the Cape Town breeze, there was a long silence on the steps of the orphanage. Then we moved back inside, slowly.

I saw Daddy Ochberg glance at Mr. Bobrow, raising his eyebrows in an exaggerated movement and cocking his head toward all of us with a concerned look. Mr. Bobrow nodded back seriously.

"We can almost fit in now," Itzik commented.

Daddy Ochberg brightened. "Time for a story!" he announced. We looked at him with interest as he settled himself on a narrow little mattress and leaned back against the wall. "Do you know the story of the man who complained that his house was too small?" he asked, patting the bed next to him to invite us to gather close.

"Tell us," Yankel shouted.

"Once there was a man," Daddy Ochberg began, "who lived in a tiny house with his wife and ten children.

"One day he complained to the rabbi of the town. 'There is no room in my house for me to move around.' The rabbi thought for a while and then he said, 'Bring your donkey into the house with you.'

"The man was amazed but he could not disobey the rabbi, so he led the donkey into the house and gave it some of the family's precious space. A few days later he complained to the rabbi. 'Rabbi, now there is no room in my house for me to eat.'

"The rabbi considered the problem and then told the man to bring his goats into the house, too. The man was in despair, but he did as the rabbi advised.

"After a day or two he complained again. 'Rabbi, now there is no room in my house for me to think.' 'Take your goats out of the house,' the rabbi replied.

"The man did so and marveled at the quiet and space he had gained. A few days later, the rabbi told him to take his donkey out of the house, also. 'Oy,' the man said proudly, 'what a big house I have, with so much space for my wife, my children, and myself.' "

Daddy Ochberg laughed deep from his belly and the children laughed, too, looking around at the room that now seemed just the right size.

Within a few weeks, the new rooms built by Daddy Ochberg at the back of the orphanage were complete, and the orphans were divided twelve to a room, by age group. For the first time in our lives, Nechama and I did not sleep next to each other. Excitedly, Nechama moved her things to the new room she would share with her little friends. But I tossed and turned in my bed at night. My arms felt empty. I know they can't keep all the sisters and brothers together in the same room, I thought, but Nechama needs me. That's why I came with her to South Africa.

A small number of Ochberg children left the Cape Jewish Orphanage during those early weeks. Two girls and a boy had cousins far north in Rhodesia; letters had arrived inviting them to come and live in the copper-mining towns. Three toddlers were adopted by Jewish families in Cape Town who couldn't have their own children. Itzik and another big boy were sent to the country to live with a Jewish shopkeeper and a Jewish farmer.

Itzik had been in the orphanage in Pinsk when Nechama and I arrived there. He was the first boy to admire me, in my flour-bag apron in Warsaw. Of all the people in the world except Nechama, I'd known him and Mr. Bobrow the longest.

I listened anxiously as Daddy Ochberg read Itzik's letters aloud. He wrote to say that he was earning a small amount of money working in his new family's general store after school every day. "My plan is to save up and open my own shop when I turn eighteen," he wrote. "I work long hours, but Mr. Katz is a fair boss. Mrs. Katz is very kind to me and a wonderful cook."

I was relieved to hear Itzik sounding so well and happy. And I was glad that no more children were sent away. After three weeks in the orphanage, I felt as if we had lived there for three months. The big building was already home.

I loved London and the ship, I remembered one night, reaching down to touch the boxes of books still housed, at Mr. Ochberg's instruction, under my bed. But I think I like Cape Town even more. It's colorful and warm and safe. No more pogroms, no more hunger, no more sickness. And I see Nechama at breakfast every morning. It is good here. I hope Mama and Papa know that.

# SAFE
## 1921

"If you are going to succeed in your new country," Daddy Ochberg told us seriously one night when he joined us for dinner, "you need to learn better English. You will be outsiders here until you laugh in English, play in English, dream in English."

I agreed silently. English is the key. I have to learn perfect English so that I can take care of Nechama and myself in the future.

In the late afternoons, the busy principal of Cape Town Central School, Mark Cohen, would drive up to our orphanage in his sputtering old car, bringing several of his teachers with him, all of them volunteers. His method of teaching was simple.

"Let's go," he called, waving his arms. When he had all of us, big and small, crowded around him, he started walking. Inside, outside, he walked, pointing at things and describing them in English. "Bird!" he bellowed.

That one was easy. Mr. Bobrow had taught it to us already. But Mr. Cohen was just warming up.

"Greedy bird," he went on.

We looked at one another blankly. Did "greedy" mean that the bird digging its beak repetitively into the soil was very hungry or very patient? Or perhaps "greedy" was the name of a type of bird?

"Greedy!" he enunciated, stuffing imaginary food into his mouth until his cheeks bulged, pretending to vomit, and then eating more.

I poked Nechama. "Greedy—like you at mealtimes."

"Shiny bird," he continued, pointing at the Cape dove's magically glistening feathers, pulling out his gold fob watch and angling it to reflect the sun, then holding up his hand as if the sun were blinding him. Finally he pulled out a brand-new coin.

We stared at him for a moment and then burst into explanation among ourselves.

"Shiny, like your curls, Nechama," was my peace offering.

Mr. Cohen beamed and pointed again at the gleaming bird, digging endlessly. "The bird is greedy. The bird is shiny."

We repeated with concentration, slowly: "The bird is greedy. The bird is shiny."

I felt panicky. So much to remember and already Mr. Cohen was walking on. Dragging Nechama, I ran after him. "You're pulling me," Nechama complained.

"Come on," I urged. "It's important."

We needed more than Mr. Cohen's afternoon lessons. Soon Nechama and I, along with the other children who were twelve and younger, were told we would be going to Miss Rosa's school. Rosa van Gelderen, a Jewish woman from Holland, was the principal of an elementary school on De Villiers Street. It would be a long walk, but there was no choice. None of the other elementary schools would accept such a large group of immigrants who could not speak English.

On the first morning before school, my stomach kept heaving. "I have to be strong for Nechama," I muttered to myself as I hovered in the bathroom. "She'll be even more scared of school if she sees me like this."

But when I came out, Nechama was chattering excitedly to Mr. Bobrow. "Let's go, Devorah!" she shouted. "Mr. Bobrow is going to walk with us today to show us the way."

I began to trail after them, but Mr. Bobrow called me to the front. "Devorah, I need you to take charge of the nine-year-old girls."

Me?

"This way, Nechama, Faygele, Malke, Jente; this way, all of you," I found myself saying authoritatively. "Stay together now."

Miss Rosa had prepared her school well. "Welcome, Devorah. Welcome, Shlayma and Zeidel," a teacher greeted us warmly. "I am Miss MacKay. Please follow me to your classroom. Our pupils are looking forward to meeting you."

I checked for Nechama, only to see her following a pretty young teacher into a different room without a backward glance.

"Wel-come, Duh-vor-ah and Shhhlay-mah and Zay-dill," Miss MacKay's class chanted in singsong voices.

I lifted my eyes quickly to see if they were teasing. But most of the faces were smiling with kind curiosity.

"These are your desks right near me, and I've given you each an exercise book and pen," Miss MacKay continued. "Please sit and we will begin our day."

I was relieved to be able to scrunch down on a little bench attached to a heavy wooden desk. When I found the courage to peek around, the others were all busy with their lessons. No one was staring at me. As the minutes passed, I felt my neck and shoulders gradually relax.

Miss MacKay was generous and patient. I would have died rather than tell her that I didn't understand even half of what she was saying that first day, but she had a way of repeating explanations for the three of us very simply, in a quiet aside. I concentrated so hard that my brain felt painfully swollen inside my skull.

At last it was time to go home, and the Ochberg children gathered at the school gate to walk together. Looking at the group, I suddenly realized that in our school uniforms we could not easily be distinguished from the South African children around us. "We all look the same," I said, smiling at Nechama. "Isn't that wonderful?"

Nechama frowned doubtfully at her dull yellow

button-up dress. "Why can't we wear pretty clothes to school?" she asked. "The ones in the last donation box were beautiful. I could wear a pinafore over the blue velvet so it wouldn't get chalk or ink on it, and you would look better in red or pink than in that yellow."

"It's safe," I explained impatiently. "Don't you see how much safer it is for us to look like everyone else?"

Nechama glanced away. She never wanted to hear my warnings about danger; she didn't even seem interested in talking about the good times back home.

I straightened the flat cotton belt on my simple dress and thought about all the things I had liked at the school: the solid wooden desks with neat holes for the inkpots and long, thin "moats" for pens and pencils; the water fountain, which shot water into my mouth at the push of a pedal. Of course, I loved the books most of all. I had received eight of them to take home, eight books I did not have to share with anyone. A reader, a heavy red history book, a worn old geography atlas, a book of science experiments and another of biology, a mathematics text, a folio of music and songs, and a dictionary of Afrikaans, the other official language in South Africa. My favorite was the English reader, with little pictures at the beginning of each chapter.

The books. A new worry suddenly made me clutch them more closely. "How will we pay for all of these?" I whispered anxiously to Shlayma. But he was more interested in kicking an empty milk carton along the path.

My question was answered after lunch. Mr. Bobrow

and Matron led everyone in the job of scrubbing the dining tables and drying them with extra care. Then the adults laid out huge rolls of new brown paper, stacks of shiny white labels, and many pairs of scissors. "Your schoolbooks do not belong to you; they belong to your school and have to be returned in good condition at the end of the year," Mr. Bobrow announced. "In order to keep them clean and to strengthen the covers, each book has to be covered in brown paper, and your name must be neatly written on a white label glued to the front."

"Each book!" Faygele protested. "I have so many."

"Each book," repeated Mr. Bobrow sternly. "Now gather around while I demonstrate the correct way to turn over the corners."

We spent hours folding and wrapping brown paper carefully around our books; it was hard to cut the paper so that it fit well. And then there were the labels to be written. I loved the precision of the job and the appearance of my books covered in fresh, smooth-brushed brown paper. I even enjoyed being among all the other children doing the same task.

Every afternoon we walked home from Miss Rosa's school together, talking and teasing. The heat was blinding. I was in charge of shepherding a group of younger children and stopping the stragglers from hanging back to look longingly into the cool darkness of the little corner shops. Inside, the Indian owners sold a bewildering selection of chocolate bars and bottles of flavored milk in bright colors and packets of potatoes sliced thinly and fried to a crisp. The shops had names such as Formosa Café or Manny's Café, but the word "café" was pronounced as if it were spelled "caffy," and the shops were nothing like the one or two elegant cafés we had seen in Warsaw.

I didn't think of Warsaw often and I hardly ever thought about That Night. When I did, I changed the direction of my thoughts quickly. I had become quite good at that—since London, maybe. Yes, it was as our boat chugged into London that I had first felt open to hope. By now a couple of months in South Africa had flown by, and trouble seemed far behind. Of course I still kept a very close eye on Nechama, and of course I remembered everthing about Poland—who else was there to remember everything? (My fingers checked my pockets automatically, but I had begun keeping my photograph in my private drawer at the orphanage.)

The orphanage felt big and beautiful and warm to me. Among its generous offerings was a real library. Once a week, it was opened by blue-eyed Miss Stella, the volunteer librarian, who loved books as intensely as I did. As she walked down the orphanage corridor with her keys, calling to us like the Pied Piper, children rushed to choose the books they would borrow but especially to hear the stories she read aloud. Miss Stella knew the exact stories from the Bible that Papa had told us, and she showed me books where those stories were written. But she also read us stories about South African children having adventures in the wild bush and about lonely princesses of France and England and about pets that saved their owners' lives.

The orphanage hosted formal debates on the first Saturday night of every month, moderated by the august Judge Joseph Herbstein. All the dining tables were cleared away, and rows of temporary seats created an auditorium. A raised platform was placed at the front for the adult participants, who were usually distinguished visitors from Cape Town society. I always made sure to arrive early so that I could find a seat near this low stage.

"We know that many of you grew up in countries where it was not safe to speak your minds, where you could not vote for the best leaders," Judge Herbstein boomed one evening. "When you learn how to debate, you learn how to think and to argue. We want you to forget your fear in this wonderful country where everyone can talk and vote freely."

There was a protesting burst of loud, forced coughing from one of the distinguished visitors seated near Judge Herbstein. Startled, everyone turned to look at the man.

Judge Herbstein seemed to falter. "Where Jewish people can talk and vote freely," he said.

I understood what the interruption meant. One of the girls at school had an uncle who had been put in jail for protesting that most brown-skinned people weren't allowed to vote in South Africa. She had explained to me that only people who had been labeled white could vote, even though their ancestors had come mainly from Holland or England. Most of the people who were called black had descended from the original inhabitants of Africa and they outnumbered whites by far. But still they could not vote.

The police were very rough with people who spoke up against the unfairness, she added. In my heart I also thought it was unfair, but I was afraid to say anything.

Judge Herbstein regained his composure, and I settled back to listen. I would never be bold enough to debate whether capital punishment was moral, or whether the arts or the sciences were more important to human life, or whether women or men were more intelligent, but I could at least vote for the best speakers.

One Saturday night, three ballet dancers performed for us. Nechama loved everything about them: their grace, their elegance, their costumes. She clapped wildly, her pretty face aglow under her mop of curls. For days afterward, she stood in front of the long mirror in the entrance hall, stretching her arms above her head while trying to spin around gracefully. As I watched, I suddenly noticed how much taller my sister had become. She looked like a young girl, not a plump child any longer. I reached out and tried to give her a hug, but Nechama pushed me away. "Stop that," she said. "I'm just getting this ballet step right."

Sundays were free days, and the tennis courts and soccer and cricket fields were full, as people in South Africa seemed to be very enthusiastic about sports. Here

Ne-chama and I were in agreement. Neither of us could understand why anyone would want to chase after a ball and hit it with something. Nechama would rather spend hours with her girlfriends trying on the torn bridal gown and high heels they had found in the dress-up box in the playroom. I lay and read books outside in the shade of the eucalyptus trees, grass blades tickling my skin and the heavy scents of oleander and hibiscus filling my nose. Often I looked up to watch the sun striking a flint on Table Bay, light shooting from the blue ocean.

The golden moments were Daddy Ochberg's visits every Friday afternoon before Shabbes dinner at the orphanage. As his big car turned into the driveway, children gathered like magnets, flying to meet him. We clung to his fingers or pinched the cloth of his jacket until he was weighed down with us and had to slop along heavily, taking ages to progress up the stairs to the front door. Nechama hung on with the rest, shrieking with laughter. And I held on to her, and the children holding on to me were also holding on to Daddy Ochberg, so that we were linked in a circle. I was happy. I had no idea that the circle was about to break.

# "How Can They Do This?"
## 1921

The day that my happiness stopped growing was a Monday. It was early December, two and a half months after we had arrived in Cape Town. The summer heat was reaching its peak, and it took us longer and longer to drag ourselves home from school.

"I'm going to put my head under the garden tap at the bottom of the driveway," Nechama declared, wiping away the sweat that collected beneath her straw hat.

"You'll get your school uniform wet and Matron will be cross. Do what I'm doing: blow upward with your lips to fan your face," I advised her.

Nechama giggled at the wisps of hair drifting up and down above my eyes, but she copied me. She still had that habit.

We reached the orphanage at last, crossing the royal purple carpet of fallen jacaranda flowers just within the gates and hurrying toward our lunch in the dark cool dining room.

"Oh good, melktert for dessert," Nechama murmured as she caught sight of a maid carrying plates of sweet custard pie on a large tray. "That means we won't be having meat for the main course, though. I like lamb chops . . . and steak and chicken, too."

"You little piggy." I laughed. "You like dairy foods, too. You even liked the baked fish in cheese that Cook tried on us last week. I think you just like *food*."

We ate well at the orphanage and never quite got used to having meat at least once a day and as much fruit as we wanted. Dessert was served after every supper, and three times a week it was served after lunch, too. There were stewed apricots with yellow custard; bread and butter pudding with a crusty meringue on top; English trifle made with cake pieces softened in jelly and whipped cream; and—my favorite—hot round crumpets served with melted butter and Lyle's Golden Syrup.

On that Monday, however, we never ate the melktert. Just before dessert, Matron appeared in the door of the dining room. She had finished her weekly meeting with the members of the Governing Board of the orphanage. She was a kind but extremely busy woman. "Nechama, Devorah, I need to talk to you in my office, please," she called firmly over the hubbub of voices.

Nechama and I gave each other puzzled looks as we pushed our chairs back and followed her. Were we in trouble? Nechama chattered too much in school, and I had lost my school hat for a short while the previous week, but Matron didn't usually call children into her office for such small offenses.

Matron sat down rather heavily behind her large desk, which was stacked with carefully arranged files. Framed photographs of groups of children hung on the walls, each one with a different year printed underneath. Nechama and I had each been given our own copy of the most recent photo, in which we stood at opposite corners of our group.

"Please be seated, Devorah and Nechama," Matron said formally, and pointed to two tall chairs still warm from the board members who had sat there.

We perched ourselves awkwardly. I felt the twitch begin in my eyelid, and I pressed a finger to my eye to try to stop it.

"As you know," Matron began, folding her hands on the desk in front of her, "soon after you arrived, eight of our children were lucky enough to be offered homes by relatives or families. We were sad to see them go, but we are very grateful that they will grow up in private homes with loving new parents."

I sat dead still, but my mind raced ahead of Matron at the speed of light. A family, a home. Were we going to have those things again? Would we have Shabbes together, and jokes and laughter? Could it be?

"Mr. and Mrs. Stein wrote to us the week after your ship arrived. They wanted a little boy at first," Matron went on. "But there was a mistake and all the boys of the age they wanted were sent to the orphanage in Johannesburg. When they came to the ballet performance last month, they saw Nechama in the audience and they changed their minds. They have chosen a girl. Nechama."

I stared blankly at Matron, but Matron was looking only at my sister.

"Yes, they chose you, Nechama," she said. "The board asked if they would take two girls, both of you, but the Steins want only one. I know the separation will be hard for both of you at first, but you'll still see each other, and Devorah can visit you in your new home and—"

Matron's voice came to a stop and there was silence in the room. I felt frozen rigid, numb. I felt again like the Devorah who had awakened the morning after That Night. Nechama looked from one face to the other. She didn't seem to understand. Matron cleared her throat and then addressed herself again to Nechama.

"I'm sure Devorah will be happy for you when she gets used to the idea," Matron said with a smile that did not reach her eyes. "This is a wonderful opportunity for you, Nechama. Louis Stein owns one of the biggest ladies' tailoring shops in town, and he and his wife have a beautiful home. She is on the Women's Committee for our orphanage and has raised a good deal of money for us among her friends."

Matron stood up from her chair. "You may go now, girls, and spend some time together. Mr. and Mrs. Stein will be here tomorrow to take Nechama to her new home." We slid off our chairs with a simultaneous thud and slipped from the room. Neither of us had said a word. I heard Matron sigh. Then the door closed.

As soon as we were out of sight, I grabbed Nechama's hand and pulled her through the front door toward some tall bushes a distance away. Nechama almost lost her footing, but I dragged her frantically. Behind the bushes we would be completely hidden.

Once there, I wheeled her around to face me. "We have to leave here right now. We have to grab our things and run away right now."

Nechama's eyes widened in horror. "But we don't have anywhere to go. We don't have any money."

"Never mind money, Nechama. Don't you under-stand? We're in terrible danger again. They're tearing us apart. We have to run. Fast, like on That Night."

"No," she whimpered. Then she pulled away. "I'm too scared out there. We're only little. We can't live alone outside."

I glared at her in rage and fear. She was right; we couldn't run away. I couldn't take care of her alone. I had failed. I had forgotten to look out for danger and it had found me unaware, unprepared. I had no money, I hadn't learned enough in school yet, I didn't even know my way around Cape Town.

I threw myself to the grass. Tears poured down my

cheeks, burning hot like a volcano. "Mama! Papa!" I called. "They're taking her away from me. Don't let them do it!"

Nechama knelt next to me and sobbed loudly, too.

I pounded the ground with my fists. "How can they do this? After we survived everything together . . ."

"You're scaring me!" Nechama cried, and I held her tightly, our cheeks slippery wet. We clung together, moaning. But no one heard us.

After a long time, I couldn't cry anymore. My fists hurt from beating at the ground. The ground was too hard; I couldn't make a mark. I felt so drained, so helpless. Nechama's fingertips dropped out of my own.

Finally, it was Nechama who searched for a handkerchief in my pocket and wiped both of our faces with it. Then she patted my back with her little hand. "Devorahleh," she said softly, "don't worry, we will still see each other sometimes."

"Sometimes!" I broke into fresh sobs of frustration, kicking wildly at the grass.

That made Nechama cry again, too, but soon she grew quiet. "It might be nice," she began thoughtfully, "to live in a beautiful house and have a new mother and father." Her hand continued to pat me a bit absently.

I sat up in one fast movement. "You're *mine*," I whispered fiercely. "There's no one else in our family. They can't tear us apart."

She dropped her chin and pulled at a dandelion.

A brilliant idea struck me. I grabbed her wrists.

"Nechama, I've got it. You must tell them you won't go. If you kick and scream enough, they won't want you and they'll choose someone else. You have to tell Matron you don't want to go. Let's go tell her right now."

Nechama dissolved into tears and pulled her hands from me to cover her face. "I can't say that to Matron, I can't!" she cried.

"Why not?" I demanded.

"Because . . . because . . . Matron will be cross with me," she ventured through her fingers.

There was something about the way she wouldn't look at me. A terrible suspicion seeped like poison into my brain. "Nechama Lehrman," I said slowly, forcing each word out of my mouth. "I think you want to go to those new people. I think you want to leave me."

"I don't! I don't!" cried Nechama.

What did she mean? What was she really saying? Surely I just had to push her a little, force her to face the truth, and she would come to her senses. "I think you want to leave us all, Mama and Papa and me," I dared to venture. "I think you want to forget everything and start again as if nothing had ever happened to us."

Her only answer was violent sobbing. I waited, but I knew already—I would not get the passionate denial I needed. My heart hurt me as it drummed under my tight ribs. I folded my arms against the pain.

"We're a family, Nechama," I said in a hoarse whisper. "We're the only ones left of our family. I promised Mama that I would take care of you. How can I take care of the family if we are apart?"

Nechama sniffed loudly. She didn't have any answer.

And then, for the first time, I gave up. I flopped down onto the grass and curled into a ball on my side. My arms had no strength left in them. "It's finished," I said. "I tried so hard, Mama, Papa, but I can't do it. There is nothing I can do now."

# "I HAVE SOME NEWS FOR YOU"
## 1921–22

After Nechama skipped away from the orphanage, looking back only once, the days passed very slowly for me. I sat on my bed for hours, thinking of nothing, or stared out the window at the hot garden with its strange, too-bright plants. First Mama and Papa had left me; then I had lost Aunt Friedka and Madame Engel. Now Nechama had gone off with strangers she was ready to call her parents. I felt as heavy as a stone. One night I dreamed that I was Papa, pulling the laden cart behind me. When I woke up in the morning, the weight hardly seemed to lift.

Daddy Ochberg and Mr. Bobrow were concerned about me, I could see that, but I took pleasure in their worry. Resentment boiled in me. How dare they separate my sister and me? Hadn't we suffered enough? And how could Nechama possibly bear to leave me? Then the anger burnt out and I sat picking at the threads in the bedspread, feeling numb.

At school, my fury served me well. I felt it pushing me, driving me to learn. I had to find out how to speak and read English perfectly, to add numbers and understand money, to know about cities and people around the world. Then I would be stronger. Then I would be able to take better care of myself. Then maybe I could get my sister back.

Nechama was doing well, I was told. The Steins had given her an English version of her name, Naomi. And she was attending a fancy private school near her new home. When I asked to see her, the grownups said it was best to let a few weeks go by first. To give her time to adapt, they said.

But what about me? Every morning, every night, there was an empty space next to me that my sister had once filled. For twenty-one days I ached for her, ached to touch her curls and see her eyes and hear her laugh. And yet I hated her.

At last Nechama-now-called-Naomi came to collect me for a visit to her new home. I was waiting for her just inside the big doors of the orphanage, my palms sweating. When I saw her halo of curls, I forgot my anger. Without a word, we clung to each other, mercifully alone in the dim entrance hall.

"Devorahleh," she murmured.

A driver in a uniform waited in the car outside. We held hands in the back of the car all the way, and my sister found her tongue again. I barely listened, conscious only of her soft little fingers in mine, the fine leather fragrance of the car, the suburbs we were reaching too quickly. I wanted the drive to last forever. But soon we had pulled up outside a large, handsome home and I was being welcomed by bluff, joking Mr. Stein and delicate, elegant Mrs. Stein. Naomi, they kept calling her. Naomi. Naomi. I was to call her Naomi, too.

Naomi herself seemed oblivious to my awkwardness. "Come to my room, Devorah," she chirped. "Come and see how pretty and pink everything is, and look at my bird in its cage. You can hold my doll. Isn't she beautiful?"

We entered a pink dream of a room and I took the heavy doll obediently. Naomi had vowed in London that she was going to have a fancy doll one day; I wished I could have been the one to give it to her. I examined the huge, rigid doll from its fancy hat down to its black patent leather pumps. "It's got lovely clothes," I said finally, "but I don't think the face is as pretty as the ones on the dolls Papa gave us." I smiled, but Naomi looked puzzled.

"At home," I prodded her. "Remember the dolls with yellow hair and blue eyes? We each had one and we used to play with them under the quilt on the big bed."

"I don't remember," Naomi said, turning to something else. "Come and look at my hand mirror with silver rosebuds carved on it. It belonged to a great-aunt who was also called Naomi—see the *N* on the back?"

So that was where my sister's new name had come from—a "great-aunt" who wasn't related at all. My anger rose. Was it really possible that she didn't remember the dolls?

"Necham—Naomi, please listen to me," I blurted. "I'm your real family. These people aren't your real family. Tell them you want to go back and live with me. Tell them you want to go home."

Naomi turned to me and I saw incredulity in her eyes. Then she gave a winsome smile and stroked my hand.

"But I like this home," she said softly. "It's prettier than the orphanage and everyone spoils me. I do miss you at night, Devorahleh, but I don't want to leave here. Can't you ask them to adopt you, too?"

"They won't," I muttered. "I've asked Matron already." I didn't elaborate on the humiliating conversation we'd had just after my sister left, in which Matron told me sadly that she'd implored the Steins to take both of us, but they had insisted that they wanted only one daughter. Like wanting only one cake, or one dress.

Naomi squeezed my hand in sympathy. Then she darted across the room and brought some exquisite doll clothes to show me, like a mother trying to distract a child.

After a few minutes of Naomi's chatter and my brief, sullen replies, a brass bell echoed through the house. "That means lunch is ready," Naomi interpreted. "Let's go. Everything tastes so, so good here."

I followed her silently, my feet sinking into the thick cream-colored carpeting, until we entered a cheerful green dining room with white-trimmed French windows leading to the garden.

"Look, Devorah," Naomi called, dancing up to a place lovingly decorated with freshly picked grapevines and white daisies and jasmine. "This is your chair."

"It was Naomi's idea. She picked everything in the garden herself," Mrs. Stein said proudly, and Mr. Stein teased my sister about how carefully she had chosen the decorations to match the dining room.

I felt my anger disappear. So she'd been waiting with eagerness to see me, too.

A maid in a starched uniform placed a large tureen of soup in front of Mrs. Stein and lifted off the lid. Fragrant steam filled my nose with the richness of a vivid memory. "Mama made soup with a whole chicken once," I said aloud, without thinking.

I closed my eyes and inhaled the evocative scent. Yes, I remembered it clearly. Once, for a few days, we had owned a live chicken. It squawked around our little yard, snapping pieces of potato from my fingers. Nechama was just a toddler, and she watched fearfully as she huddled behind the door and refused to step outside. On the Friday after Papa brought the chicken home from his travels, he picked it up and took it to the shochet, the community's slaughterer, to be killed. The chicken soup we had that night for Shabbes was a heavenly pool, glistening with golden suns.

"Oh, Mama," I had said. "It's so much nicer than your usual chicken-feet soup."

Papa laughed. "As different as wine from grape juice,

Devorahleh."

Mama beamed. "After the soup, we will eat the chicken meat itself. It is so tender that it fell right off the bones." We ate the chicken meat with Mama's smooth mashed potatoes, and Nechama and I argued happily over which was softer.

I opened my eyes, only to meet Naomi's puzzled look. Mr. Stein was fiddling nervously with his napkin, and Mrs. Stein still had her soup ladle poised in the air.

"Um, would you like some of . . . Cook's soup, Devorah? She makes it very well and Naomi loves it."

"No," I heard myself say. I did not say thank you and I squeezed the edge of the tablecloth until my fingers were sore, determined to stop myself from crying through the rest of the uncomfortable meal.

Mr. Stein drove me home quite soon after lunch, and that night I lay in bed sleepless. What now? I cried silently, the tears running down my face and pooling in my ears. What now?

Two more months passed, and I wilted in the glare of my first South African summer. Near the end of February, the crows cawed faintly in the heat. I was in English class, absorbed in memorizing a poem. I heard a tapping sound, and saw Daddy Ochberg knocking lightly at the little window set into the door of the classroom.

Miss MacKay hurried to the door to talk with him. I bent my head over my poem again, chewing on the tip of my thick braid.

"Devorah!" Miss MacKay called. "Mr. Ochberg says he can take you home in his car, so you can leave a little early today. Pack your books, and remember your hat and blazer."

I felt myself flush with surprise and pleasure as I hurried to get ready. It was a treat to be alone with Daddy Ochberg; usually children were fighting to skip next to him and hold his hand.

I chattered about school while we drove toward the orphanage. Daddy Ochberg smiled, but he didn't say much and he seemed distracted, as if he wasn't really listening. Gradually I began to feel uneasy. When we reached the building, Daddy Ochberg parked at the side rather than in front of the big doors.

"Let's go into the garden, Devorah," he said. "I have some news for you."

He took my hand and led me onto the quiet lawn. We walked for a few moments in silence; my eyelid started to twitch. Daddy Ochberg coughed, started to say something, hesitated, then began determinedly. "Devorah, there is a couple who want to adopt you."

I stopped still and stared at him.

"Their name is Kagan and they are nice people. Mr. Kagan is a photographer. He was very ill a few years ago; he had a disease called tuberculosis. But his doctor says he is better now and it is safe for you to be with him."

Daddy Ochberg kept a firm hold on my hand and

continued his slow pacing up and down the lawn, leading me along. "I want to explain to you, Devorah. They are not rich people. You will always have enough to eat and you will have warm clothes. You will keep going to school, I'll see to that, and you'll go to synagogue with them. But there will not be money for luxuries; they are not rich people. Do you understand?"

My head was pulsing; so much information to sort out. A family wanted me; I would have a family again. Nice people. But Daddy Ochberg hadn't sounded too certain. The man had a sickness with a complicated name, something you could catch, like the typhoid. What did it mean that they were not rich? It must be important. Daddy Ochberg had said it twice.

I heard myself blurt one silly question out of the jumble in my head: "Do they have a maid like the Steins have?"

Daddy Ochberg looked surprised. "Yes, I think they have a maid, Devorah Lehrman. Most white people in South Africa do have servants, you know. Is that what's important to you, little one?"

My eyes filled with tears at the misunderstanding, and Daddy Ochberg let go of my hand and put his arms around me. He picked me up right off the ground and gave me a hug before putting me down.

"It will be good for you to have parents again, Devorah. You've had to look after yourself for too long, as well as take care of your sister. She now has a family, and we think you need one, too."

I clenched my fists. He spoke as if Naomi and I were separate now, as if Naomi didn't need me anymore.

Daddy Ochberg was talking again, briskly. "I have to hurry off now. Matron knows that I've explained things to you. Next month I'll come and visit you at the Kagans' house." We were back at the big front door, and he deposited my schoolbag next to me. "I'm glad for you, Devorah. And I think you'll be glad for yourself one day." Then he was walking back to his car, turning with a smile and a wave before he closed the car door.

I took a step after him. My eyelid was flickering. Questions tangled in my head. But Daddy Ochberg started the car and drove away, down the driveway and out of the orphanage.

I sat on my bed until supper, staring at the floor without seeing anything. When the bell rang for the evening meal, I went downstairs slowly. All around me, the others ate and talked happily, but the food wouldn't go down my throat.

"Devorah." Matron called me aside after supper. "Too excited to eat, dear? Now, I want you to pack your clothes and books in the morning. You won't go to school tomorrow because your new parents will be here at noon."

I flinched. New parents! What did that make my "old" parents? And what about my sister? Was she going to give me a new sister, too?

Suddenly I had an idea. "Matron, will you speak to the Steins?" I blurted. "Will you speak to the Steins and tell them I'm going to a family now, so Naomi must come and be with me because she's my sister. I'm sure the Kagans will take Naomi; she's so sweet and pretty. I'll beg until they agree. Put us together again, please, Matron."

Matron sighed and put her arm around me. "You know the Steins would never give Naomi up, dear. They love her. She's their daughter now."

I wanted to kick and scream as I'd urged Naomi to do. I wanted to run out the door, walk all the way to Naomi's house, grab her by the arm, and run away with her. But I just looked down while Matron gave me advice about manners and appreciation and keeping neat and tidy.

Finally I was released. "Why don't you go to sleep now, Devorah," Matron said with another hug. "You'll be up early in the morning, I'm sure. Have a good night, dear."

But the night wasn't good; it was long and black and full of nightmares about Mama and Papa. Mama and Papa kept asking me where my sister was, and I didn't know the answer. They kept asking me not to forget them, and they didn't seem to hear my replies. I called and called to them, but their dim figures turned away from me and were swallowed by the darkness.

# THE KAGANS
## 1922

On the morning of February 28, 1922, I gathered together my belongings, my hands moving like those of a mechanical puppet I'd seen in London. I pulled back my dark hair and tied it so severely that my forehead felt stretched. I didn't know what to wear, so I put on my school uniform. When I looked in the mirror, I saw that my face was tired and peaked, with two bright spots flushing my cheekbones.

I was ready long before noon, sitting straight up on the neat bed, my battered English suitcase on the ground. More than ever before, my bed, the dormitory room with its row of identical beds, and the windows looking out onto the garden felt secure and familiar.

"I'm afraid," I whispered into the silence. My stomach was tight as a drum as I waited to be summoned, but by ten past twelve no one had come to the door or called my name. Eventually I stood up and peered down the hallway. One of the older girls, Chava, was hurrying from the direction of Matron's office.

When she saw me she scowled and called out irritably, "Hurry, Devorah, Matron's waiting for you and she's cross."

"I've been ready," I squeaked. "I thought I was supposed to—"

But there wasn't time to explain. Chava snatched up my suitcase and hurried back down the hallway. I followed, my eyes prickling at the unfairness.

At Matron's office, Chava opened the door and gave me a little push inside. I stumbled awkwardly into the room and opened my mouth. I wanted to say that I had been ready, that I had been waiting in the dormitory. But Matron was tapping her pencil on the desk and she didn't give me a chance.

"Finally, there you are. Devorah, meet Mr. and Mrs. Kagan, who have very kindly adopted you. This is Devorah Lehrman."

A tall man got up from the edge of the chair where he was perched and came toward me with his hand outstretched. His long, thin arms and legs made him look like a huge gangling spider, and I shrank back. But his voice was gentle as he took my hand. "Hello, my dear. We're very glad to meet you."

Then I felt myself being pulled against a corseted, substantial bosom and kissed firmly on the top of my head. A large woman with a florid face and beads of sweat on her upper lip beamed at me.

"You need some fattening up, poor child. Nearly starved in that terrible country. Going to see to it, get some good food in you now. All you have, that one little suitcase? That's all, Matron? All the papers signed at last? So many papers. And in this heat. Affects me worse every year. All right, come along now, Mr. Kagan. Get this little one home, shall we?"

In a burst of half sentences, and trailing Mr. Kagan and me behind her, Mrs. Kagan bustled to the door, thanked Matron, and set off down the long driveway. I looked back helplessly. Goodbye, Cape Jewish Orphanage, goodbye. Another goodbye.

The next few hours spun by dizzily, propelled by Mrs. Kagan's brisk bossiness and energy. It wasn't until the end of the day, when I was finally alone in the room I was to call my own, that I had time to sort through the startling changes in my life.

The Kagans lived in a flat in a three-story building about twenty minutes' walk from the orphanage. There wasn't much space and my room wasn't really a room, more like a large walk-in cupboard under the stairs to the upstairs neighbor. But it had been vigorously cleaned until the floorboards shone and the little window gleamed. There was a pretty yellowwood washstand backed with six green tiles, and a woven rug next to the bed. I was glad to sit down on the white knobby bedspread, rest my elbows on my knees and my head on my hands, and think for a while.

My thoughts went first to Mr. Kagan. I liked him, but of course not in the way I had liked my own father. Mr. Kagan wasn't strong and fun, he wasn't someone who could toss you up to his shoulders or silence you with a single look when you had been too noisy. He was very quiet, timid maybe; his voice was gentle and his light blue eyes were soft and droopy, like a puppy's eyes. Mrs. Kagan must have thought so, too, because she treated him just like a favorite dog. She told him where to go and what to do, and once I saw her stroke the fine hair on his head indulgently.

Her own dark blond hair was carefully arranged in waves and sprayed so that the waves never shifted. A thick layer of powder sat on the reddish skin of her cheeks, and when she perspired, the powder gathered in moist wrinkles. And yet her face was kind.

I couldn't decide about Mrs. Kagan yet. She was big and solid, and she moved like the three girls at my school who sometimes linked arms and plowed through the crowds on the playground chanting: "We. Walk. Straight. So. You'd-Better-Get-Out-of-the-Way." She seemed to me like a strong wind, almost a storm. She made you want to brace yourself and stand firm, so you wouldn't blow over. I had to smile a little: it seemed clear that Mr. Kagan had lain right down when that wind first hit him.

"Cleaned this room out for you myself on the weekend, so no need to worry about spiders," she had said as her busy hands shoved the little bed close up against the wall and straightened the towel hanging on the washstand. Then she had insisted on helping me unpack my small suitcase. When the few clothes were lifted out and she saw my old photograph packed carefully at the bottom, Mrs. Kagan suffocated me for a moment in a massive hug.

"We'll take care of you now, dearie. Climb in bed and get a good night's sleep." With a kiss on the top of my head and a bang of the door, she was gone, leaving quiet in her wake.

I guessed that the Kagans were sitting together on the hard, overstuffed couch in the living room, a room heavy with framed photographs taken by Mr. Kagan. There were photographs of white brides, stiff Bar Mitzvah boys, plump babies, and unsmiling grandparents.

"Will I be related to all these people now—now that you've adopted me?" I had asked.

Mrs. Kagan, straightening an ornate frame, had laughed. "Oh, none of these people are Kagans, my dear. I don't know any of them at all."

I gazed around the living room, surrounded by strangers. But Mrs. Kagan bustled on. She was very proud of her husband's photography and showed me his tiny darkroom at the back of the flat as if it were a stateroom for a king. It was a scary place, I thought, very dark and smelling of chemicals. There were buckets of shiny liquid and clothespins on long cords that brushed my hair like cobwebs.

"Does Mr. Kagan work in here every day?" I asked.

Mrs. Kagan's cheeks grew pinker and she said a little too loudly, "Mr. Kagan used to have a large photographic studio in Stellenbosch . . ." She looked closely at me and gave the specific address as if I was daring to disbelieve her. "Muller's Buildings on Plein Street in Stellenbosch. But his talent was not appreciated. Not fully appreciated by those . . . farmers. Anyway, Mr. Kagan's health was not good at the time. Quite well now, thank God. So we decided it'd be best for him not to bother with the public but to do photo developing right here. Yes, at home on Caledon Street."

She shut the door of the darkroom carefully before showing me the rest of the small flat. It consisted of the living room with an alcove for a dining table, Mr. and Mrs. Kagan's bedroom, a bathroom with a very short but deep tub on clawed feet, and my own room under the stairs. There was also a steamy little kitchen, where a black woman named Elizabeth smiled at me and wished me welcome.

"Nice to have three places at the table, my dear," Mrs. Kagan boomed as we sat down to eat dinner in the dining alcove. Mr. Kagan, too, gave a sweet smile before turning his full attention to the cabbage leaves wrapped around ground beef and rice and onions.

"Another helping, Devorah? Elizabeth's stuffed cabbage is very good; couldn't do better myself." I was just about to agree when Mrs. Kagan, her big serving spoon hovering, went on. "You must be very hungry, my dear. Poor orphans, starving in the streets. Well, you won't go hungry here."

Suddenly the pity in Mrs. Kagan's voice felt unbearable. She wasn't the only person in the world to give me meals. My mama and papa had fed me very well for many years and after that they'd done the best they could. Madame Engel had seated me like a princess in her huge restaurant kitchen. And I'd had plenty of delicious food at the orphanage before Mrs. Kagan marched me away. I wasn't a starving child on the street! "I don't need another helping, thank you," I said stiffly.

Dessert was fried bananas, and I almost smiled. If my sister had been with me, I could have whispered, "Remember the first time we saw a banana, on our bus ride from the Cape Town harbor to the orphanage?"

A wave of tiredness made me long to lie down. "Is it all right if I go to bed now?" I asked as soon as Elizabeth had removed the plates.

"Of course, dearie," said Mrs. Kagan. "Want to settle in, no doubt. Say good night, Mr. Kagan." Mr. Kagan obeyed with another warm smile and a pat on my head.

Now I sat on the bed staring straight ahead of me, without the energy to move. Beyond the wall, Mr. Kagan coughed and the sound moved me to action. I put on the faded green nightdress Matron had distributed to me in the orphanage, brushed my teeth at the nightstand, and washed my face.

Then I went to the little window to say the Shema the way my mama used to. She had always stood quietly for a moment and gazed out at the night before she began. She covered her eyes for the first important line, to concentrate better: "Hear, O Israel, the Lord is our God, the Lord is One." Then she continued softly to the end. And I next to her.

Never, except on the Night of the Burning, had I forgotten to say the Shema before I slept. Since That Night I had added a personal thank-you to Aunt Friedka.

"Mama," I whispered. "Mama and Papa, are you up there?"

The night blinked with its many eyes.

"Mama and Papa, I'm in my new home, but it's not my real home and I'll never forget you. I will love you forever."

Then I climbed into the bed. It was a warm night in the middle of summer, but someone had taken the care to wrap a hot brick in felt and place it between the sheets for my feet. I had never had my own heating brick before, and it felt luxurious and warm against my toes.

It may be all right here. I'll wait and see, I decided, weariness pulling me deep down into sleep.

## "I Want My Mama"
### 1922

When I woke up the next morning, the first thing I noticed was the silence. Where was the commotion of children's voices, laughing and shouting and racing to get to the bathroom first? I scrambled off the bed and pulled on my school dress again. Then I opened my door and peered out. The only sounds came from the kitchen, so I walked slowly in that direction.

Elizabeth stood at the sink, washing dishes. She was wearing an apron over her blue uniform dress. A matching blue scarf was tied around her neatly shaped head and knotted behind her neck.

"Good morning, Miss Devorah," she said to me with a quiet smile. Her high cheekbones were like little round apples. "I will make your breakfast." She pointed to a small kitchen table where a single place had been laid. I sat down.

"Where are—" I said and then stopped. I didn't know what to call Mr. and Mrs. Kagan.

Elizabeth had her own titles for them. "The master is working in his darkroom, and the madam has gone to buy more milk and bread," she said.

I was distracted by the tempting smell of the toast placed in front of me. At my side a plate of creamy porridge steamed, butter melting in the middle and sugar sprinkled on the top. I ate hungrily.

Elizabeth seemed to have finished her work for a while. She sat down on a step stool, one arm folded across her stomach and the other hand supporting her cheek. (I'd noticed that when the black staff at the orphanage were not working, they could sit very still for long periods. As if they were waiting for something that might not come for a long time.) Then she began to sing a song to herself, in a pleasant soft voice that I liked.

Suddenly my ear caught a name. Jesus Christ the Lord, she was singing, Jesus Christ our Savior. I dug my fingers into my palms. The song was about the god of the Polish peasants. If Elizabeth believed in that god, maybe she hated Jews. I was close to the door. Should I slip away quietly and stay near Mr. Kagan? But maybe I wasn't allowed to interrupt him when he was working.

It was a relief to hear Mrs. Kagan return noisily, bursting open the front door and marching into the kitchen.

"Devorah, dear, having breakfast? Good. Nothing like porridge. Mail arrive yet, Elizabeth? A cup of tea for me, please. Nearly fainted in this heat."

She walked into the little dining area and sat down heavily, fanning her face vigorously. I trailed after her.

"Matron up at the orphanage said you're a good student, Devorah," she announced. "Mr. Kagan and I were proud to hear that. Wasn't much of a student myself. Which subject d'you like best?"

I answered absently, "English . . . I like English class." Then I took a breath and asked, "What must I call you?"

Mrs. Kagan stopped drinking her tea for a moment. "You can call us Mother and Father, dearie. Children nowadays don't seem to say Mama and Papa."

I stared at her. This large, red-faced woman slurping her cup of tea? Mother?

My horror must have been visible, because Mrs. Kagan looked as though someone had smacked her. Her jaw hung for a moment and then she said stiffly, "At least, that is what we would like. You can do as you wish, of course."

She heaved to her feet and went down the hallway, shouting loudly to Mr. Kagan that she was back home. I sat quite still. I had hurt Mrs. Kagan's feelings, that was clear. But I can't call her by that name, I thought. I just can't.

Later that day, Mrs. Kagan took me to a shop

downtown to buy a new school uniform.

"Can't wear that worn-out old thing when you go back to school tomorrow," she announced. "You're not an orphanage girl anymore. Not going to wear a faded second-hand uniform that someone donated."

Before I knew what was happening, I was fitted with a new yellow dress for summer, and a gray flannel skirt, two white shirts, and a school tie for winter. With them went a new hat, a cardigan, a navy blazer, and even regulation panties and socks. A pristine brown school case completed the ensemble. The clothes felt starched and smooth; they were newer and more expensive than anything I had ever owned before. I turned around in front of the mirror with wonder. Then I saw Mrs. Kagan carefully counting out the money at the cash register. I blushed at causing the Kagans such expense.

"Thank you very much," I said softly on the way home.

Mrs. Kagan beamed at me. "It's a pleasure, dearie. Want you to look just like the other girls."

Just like the other girls. I tried to read her face. Did Mrs. Kagan also know about the dangers of being conspicuous?

The next day I returned to school, self-conscious but proud in my new clothing.

"You came back to our school," Zeidel greeted me with surprise. "I thought you'd go to a posh private school like your sister."

Little Faygele rushed up with a warm hug. "Ooh, your

clothes are so new," she said. "You lucky duck."

"What's your family like? Do you have your own room?" asked Shlayma.

"Did they buy toys for you, too?" asked Faygele.

My cheeks burned with the attention. "They're fine. Yes, I sleep alone. No, just the school clothes." I would never admit to them that I'd trade a million new dresses to be back in the orphanage along with my sister.

Zeidel fingered the neat label on my new school case. "Why do you still call yourself Devorah Lehrman?" he asked. "Don't you have a new name now?"

I frowned. I didn't want a new name, would never agree to one. But I had been surprised when Mrs. Kagan wrote Devorah K. Lehrman. If she was going to take me into her family, shouldn't she make Kagan my last name, not just my middle initial? Oh, I didn't care.

I was in the highest grade at Miss Rosa's elementary school, and I would have to go to a strange new school, a high school, the following year. But for now at least, school was the same. Miss MacKay was telling us about the Great Trek, when thousands of Afrikaans-speaking white South Africans traveled by ox wagon into the wild interior of South Africa to escape English domination. There were many children the same age as Nechama and I on the dangerous journey to find new land. But they had their parents with them.

I dreaded the long walk alone from school to the Kagans'. To occupy myself, I began picturing in my head, one after the other, the exact routes to the various "homes" I'd known in the last year and a half—the muddy, crooked pathways in Domachevo, the daily promenade home from Madame Engel's restaurant to our battered building in Warsaw, the enchanted streets of London that led to our grand hotel, and the long driveway up to the orphanage.

You can do it, I told myself. It will never again be as hard as this very first time. And it was true: in a few days my feet seemed to know the way back to Caledon Street on their own.

If Mrs. Kagan was at home, I would go straight to my room after lunch, work on my homework, and then sink luxuriously into the world of a library book until supper. But if Mrs. Kagan was out, I liked to sit in the kitchen for a while after I finished lunch. Elizabeth sat silently on her step stool, her feet still and parallel in worn black shoes on the bottom step. Sometimes she sighed or clicked her tongue, shaking her head with a soft "Aai."

The songs she sang didn't frighten me anymore, and after a while I even learned some of the words. But one evening Mrs. Kagan heard me singing in my bath, "Onward, Christian soldiers . . ."

"Devorah!" said Mrs. Kagan through the bathroom door.

I stopped singing abruptly.

"I never want to hear you singing about Christian soldiers again," Mrs. Kagan said angrily. "Christian soldiers have never been good for Jews, that's for sure. You hear me?"

"Yes," I answered, just loudly enough to be heard. Mrs. Kagan had never rebuked me so firmly before. My face flamed with embarrassment.

There were so many questions I wanted to ask. Why did some Christians hate Jews? And why did others not hate us? How could I know which ones to be wary of? But I just could not ask Mrs. Kagan. And there was hardly ever a chance to talk to Mr. Kagan alone. When he emerged from his darkroom or from the long rests he took in their bedroom, Mrs. Kagan was always there to fuss over him.

I didn't sing the songs myself anymore, but I still sat with Elizabeth some days. It was very peaceful in the kitchen, with the pots hissing and spitting a little on the stove. Elizabeth didn't seem happy, but she didn't seem sad, either. I thought we were quite similar, really. We didn't fit in the Kagans' home, but it wasn't a bad place to be.

Mrs. Kagan hardly ever sat quietly, and sometimes I felt my head would burst from her rapid conversation. Actually, it wasn't really conversation, because that involves two people. Mrs. Kagan could keep going for minutes at a time even if Mr. Kagan and I said not a word in response.

"Don't know what this country's coming to . . ." was a favorite beginning. Then Mrs. Kagan could swing just as easily into a speech on the price of fruit as she could into a lament about the lack of respect paid to dear King George's portrait, which hung, undusted, in the post office. When she complained about so many little black children hanging around the streets instead of going to school, I squinted toward the kitchen uncomfortably.

"Parents should be ashamed!" Mrs. Kagan would declare. "Children doing nothing but play all day. Girls wearing clothes so skimpy the boys can see their little black legs. Got to get them into uniforms and into the schools. Lot of nonsense!"

I hated it when Mrs. Kagan spoke that way near Elizabeth. How did Mrs. Kagan think someone like Elizabeth could pay for her children's school uniforms? But Mrs. Kagan never seemed to worry about whether Elizabeth was in earshot and might be offended.

While Mrs. Kagan talked, Mr. Kagan ate his dinner silently, his tall, thin frame leaning down to the food. Somehow I never minded the way he bent over his plate, his knife and fork held awkwardly in his bony hands. But my nerves screamed when Mrs. Kagan smacked her lips loudly over her food or picked her teeth with a toothpick, one little finger held high in the air in a show of daintiness.

Sometimes I just couldn't stand it. "May I be excused from the table?" I would say suddenly, pushing back my chair. "I have lots of homework to do."

Mrs. Kagan would stop in mid-sentence and look bewildered for a moment. Then she would collect herself. "That's all right, dear. Go right ahead if you've had enough to eat. Would never keep you from your schoolwork."

Mr. Kagan's little smile was apologetic as he looked

from her to me. Which of us was he apologizing to, I wondered briefly. Then I escaped to my silent room with relief.

A couple of months after I moved to Caledon Street, I woke one night with a burning sore throat. It hurt too much to call out, so I lay whimpering for a long time, staring at the strip of light under my door. Then the door opened quietly and a tall shadow appeared. It was Mr. Kagan. I didn't have the strength to wonder if he popped in every night to check if I was sleeping; I was just glad to have help nearby.

"Sore," I whispered with cracked lips. "Hot."

Mr. Kagan slipped rapidly out of the door again and I heard him calling Mrs. Kagan with urgency.

Mrs. Kagan bustled in immediately, turning on the bright light overhead. I closed my eyes. A large hand was laid firmly on my forehead.

"Fever," Mrs. Kagan announced. "Aspirin. Cold water. And some cloths."

The light was too bright, the noise too loud, the cold cloths laid on my forehead too wet. I felt wretched.

"Mama," I whispered.

"I'm right here, dear," Mrs. Kagan replied in a glad voice.

But I shook my head miserably. "I want my mama," I cried, despite my thirteen years. And cried and cried.

Now we were all wretched.

Abruptly Mrs. Kagan made a decision. "Nice cup of rooibos tea with honey and lemon. That'll do the trick," I heard her say decisively as she left. Mr. Kagan turned around twice in his helplessness and then he thought to turn off the bright lights. I pushed fretfully at the cloths trickling water from my forehead down to my neck, and he quickly removed them. Grateful, I reached out to him, and he sat close to my bed, his long, thin fingers holding my hand gently. The cloths must have cooled me down because I felt better. As I drifted into sleep, I felt a tear fall on my wrist.

It became terribly important to keep the fence up between Mrs. Kagan and myself. I had to show Mama that I wasn't going to abandon her, no matter how hard Mrs. Kagan tried to be my mother. When I saw her fleshy, freckled hands setting the table for Shabbes dinner, I remembered how Mama used to call Nechama and me to join her as she stood quietly before the candles. Mama placed a white scarf over her hair and lit the wicks. Then she moved her beautiful slim hands above the burning candles in a circle once, twice, three times and covered her face.

"Blessed art Thou, O Lord our God, King of the Universe, who has sanctified us by Thy commandments, and commanded us to light the Shabbes candles," she murmured, and we recited the blessing, too. But Mama wasn't finished. She kept her hands over her eyes for what seemed a long time, and sometimes tears slid between her fingers before she uncovered her face and kissed us.

"Why do you cry, Mama?" I asked once.

"I cry because I think how much I want you and Nechama to be happy and to be good; and I cry for my own mama and papa, may they rest in peace; and I cry for our people," she answered. At that time I didn't understand. Now that I, too, wanted to cry for the same reasons, it brought Mama and me even closer.

So when Mrs. Kagan put her arm around me after lighting the Shabbes candles, I kept my body rigid and unyielding. After a few weeks, she gave up pulling me closer.

Once Friday night dinner was over, it was obvious that the Kagans were not particular about the rules of Shabbes. Mr. Kagan would turn on the light at his reading chair, and Mrs. Kagan clicked her knitting needles busily.

"Would you like to learn how to knit, dear?" Mrs. Kagan offered brightly. "My mother taught me when I was much younger than you are now."

Mama had promised to show me how to do fine embroidery when I grew old enough. It would be disloyal to accept Mrs. Kagan's knitting lessons as a substitute. "No, thanks, I'll just read my book," I replied.

The uncomfortable chairs made my back ache, so I tried sprawling on the rose-patterned rug, but instead of feeling relaxed I simply felt childish and undignified. "Well, maybe I'll go to my room," I said after a few minutes. "Good night."

I'm so lonely, I realized as I closed the door and sat down drearily on my bed. If only Naomi were here, we could gossip about the other orphans at the supper table, and then in the bedroom we could laugh at Mrs. Kagan's speeches. I closed my eyes and pictured my sister's gay laugh and bright face. I always thought she needed me, I admitted ruefully. I didn't know I needed her, too.

I leaned over to my nightstand and pulled out one of the three books I was reading at the same time. It took just a few moments to escape from my own life. When I had first started to read English, in London, the vivid, magical illustrations became my best friends; now, less than a year later, I needed only words to draw pictures for me of Toad, Ratty, and Badger. Then I discovered my bosom friends, two storybook girls who also didn't have mothers: the little Swiss girl, Heidi, and the first American girl I met, Rebecca of Sunnybrook Farm. The hours passed quietly, marked by the turning of pages.

# A Visit to Naomi's House
## 1922

I didn't know who was supposed to arrange my next visit with my sister. I think the orphanage assumed the adoptive families would take care of it, and maybe Mrs. Stein and Mrs. Kagan each thought the other should call and set up a date. Three months passed after I was adopted before I saw Naomi.

On the day my sister turned ten, I asked Mrs. Kagan if I could call her on the telephone. "Certainly, dear . . . show you how to . . . this telly-phone . . . always trouble . . . Hello! Operator, do you hear me? Oper-rrrrrray-ter . . ."

Mrs. Stein answered. "Hello, Devorah, how nice of you to remember the date. We are cutting Naomi's cake at this very minute. Hold the line, and I'll let her talk to you just for a moment, as we're all gathered around waiting. Oh, and Devorah, I've been meaning to call Mrs. Kagan— would you like to spend Sunday at our house? Mr. Stein will be happy to get you in his car after his tennis match."

At 11 a.m. on Sunday, I went downstairs and waited at the entrance to my building. My hands were perspiring as I clutched the little gift I'd made. A deep, rich growl announced the arrival of Mr. Stein's motorcar and, resplendent in a snowy white sweater and long white shorts that reached almost to his long white socks, he jumped out of his seat and came around to open the passenger door for me.

"Devorrrah, menorrrrah!" he sang as he drove.

I smiled awkwardly. The trouble was that I never knew when I was supposed to laugh at his teasing. I was relieved when the big black car turned into the driveway leading to the Stein home. Naomi was waving excitedly from the front door.

We caught each other in a tight hug and I closed my eyes. How I had missed the familiar tickling of her soft hair, and especially the feel of her arms around my neck. Surreptitiously, I rubbed away the wetness on my eyelashes as I followed Naomi to the pink bedroom.

Photographs were strewn across the bed, ready to be pasted into a new leather photo album. "This is me at my ballet class," Naomi pointed out. "I can't really go up on my toes alone, so Mummy is holding my hands."

I suddenly remembered Naomi on the day of the ballet performance at the orphanage. She was shining with pleasure and excitement. No wonder the Steins had wanted to take her home with them.

"And here I am with my cousins at a picnic," Naomi continued, pointing at a photograph of a big merry crowd sitting among wicker baskets on a red-checkered cloth. I murmured politely, although the family pictures made my stomach churn.

My attention was caught by the labels on some schoolbooks strewn on my sister's desk. "Naomi Stein" was printed neatly on each one. Her adoptive parents hadn't been stingy with *their* family name.

The loud brass bell rang for lunch. "Let's go!" Naomi yelped, knocking over the photographs and pulling me by the hand. "It's roast beef!"

I laughed, finding again the old exasperated love for my little sister. Naomi was still an ever-hungry puppy.

At lunch, Mrs. Stein put the choicest pieces of beef onto Naomi's plate without even trying to hide what she was doing. Mr. Stein cracked more jokes, and Naomi laughed easily at all of them. Finally he got down on his knees, pretended to be a bear, and crawled around the table to tickle her.

"Help! Help!" Naomi squealed delightedly. "Devorah, help me!"

I smiled uncertainly. What was the right thing to do? Was I supposed to join in? I was saved from deciding when suddenly Naomi's squirming knocked over a glass of water.

"Now, that's enough," Mrs. Stein said, but she was also smiling. She rang a little bell on the table and the maid appeared. "Mavis, will you bring a cloth and wipe up here, please. Mr. Stein," she ordered affectionately, "sit right back down or you won't get dessert."

Mr. Stein sat down hurriedly with a naughty face. Catching my eye, he winked. Embarrassed, I looked down at my beef and began to cut it carefully. I saw Mr. Stein lift a small silver jug and lean across to fill my glass. "How about some milk, Devorah?"

I almost choked, my eyes popping in amazement. How could I drink milk while eating beef? Surely he knew that Jews can't eat meat and milk at the same meal. It was the Law.

"Umm, no, thank you," I managed to mutter. Then I watched Mr. Stein fill Naomi's glass with milk. Without any hesitation, Naomi took a long drink. I squeezed my lips together so tightly I bit them. Didn't she remember anything at all from home?

It seemed hours until lunch was over and we were alone. Then I burst out, "How could you drink milk at lunch? You know we don't eat meat and milk together."

"We do here," was Naomi's casual answer as she sprawled on her lacy bed, surrounded by her photographs.

"We're Jews; we don't do that," I said.

"Mummy says there's no need to be too Jewish," Naomi answered.

I stared at her. No need. Too Jewish. The strange words hung in the air.

Sitting up, Naomi looked defiantly at me and said in a small, determined voice, "Maybe Mama and Papa and everyone else wouldn't have died if they weren't so Jewish."

I gasped. My brain felt paralyzed and I shook my head to clear it. I needed time to work out what she was saying, to understand how she could say such terrible things. I perched uncomfortably on the pink kidney-shaped stool of the dressing table set. Naomi wouldn't meet my eyes. There was silence. Then, with a huge effort, I started on a completely different subject. "How do you like your teacher?" I asked formally.

Naomi brightened. "I love her. She reads books and poetry to us and she talks really quietly. All the girls want to be her pet. Her leg is shrunken from an operation that went wrong, but she's very pretty."

Before I could stop myself, I said, "Mama's legs were shrunken. Before she died." My voice trailed off. Naomi wouldn't want to talk about that.

But Naomi asked with genuine interest, "Is that what she died of?"

"No, she died of typhoid fever . . . and hunger, I suppose." It was almost too painful for me to say the second part.

Naomi was quiet. Then she asked another question. "Is Daddy Ochberg our uncle?"

"Of course not. He chose us at the orphanage in Pinsk, but we hadn't met him before then. How can you not remember that?"

Naomi's lip quivered at my sharp tone, but she persevered. "We don't have any real uncles?"

I flicked scornfully at the album photos of Naomi being held by smiling men and women.

"Everyone's dead, Nechama!" I snapped. "Everyone's dead."

Perhaps it was my use of the old name; perhaps Naomi couldn't bear the anger in my voice. Burying her head in her lacy pillows, she sobbed loudly.

"Shh, don't cry," I said quickly, moving over to the bed and patting her shoulder. It was the way it used to be when I was the strong older sister drying Nechama's tears. I was glad to be back in that role.

But Naomi wasn't the same little girl. Shaking off my hand, she pulled away, snatched a lace handkerchief, and blew her nose. Then she turned to me, her swollen eyes blazing. "You make me feel bad. Like I've forgotten my family," she stormed. "But I only remember Papa a little bit, and Mama when she was sick in the bed. I've got my own mother and father now, and my own room and my own pretty things."

I opened my mouth, but Naomi wasn't finished. "I'm happy now!" she cried. "Even if you don't like it, Devorah, I'm happy here."

There was a sudden silence. Then I realized Mrs. Stein was standing in the doorway. I couldn't tell how much of the conversation she had heard, but her voice was very quiet as she said, "I think I'll take you home now, Devorah. Where did you put your coat?"

# A FRIEND
## 1923

In January 1923, when I was close to fourteen, I began attending the enormous local high school, with ivy softening its gray stone walls. Fortunately, a few students from Miss Rosa's school moved there together. We were all scared of the mazelike corridors, the blur of rushing bodies on the stairways, the loud shouts of mockery tossed like hard balls among the older students. For the first few days, we shuffled from classroom to classroom in a tight little group like a flock of sheep.

Gradually the high school revealed its wonders. Its library was almost as big as the public library branch near my home. The science laboratory had a mysterious little gas tap for each high table. Fragile glass pipettes stood like ballerinas in a row, *en pointe*, each supported at the waist by a strong wooden arm. There was an auditorium with a real stage for school plays, framed by rich red velvet curtains. And the tree-dotted lawn where we sat during lunch stretched green and immaculate down to the sports fields.

"So much homework," Shlayma complained one morning at the end of the first month. "They're giving us double the work we used to have at the old school."

Zeidel nodded. "I worked so late last night that Matron turned off the light. I wasn't even finished."

I was silent. They would think I was strange if I told them that I loved the challenge. Schoolwork was clean and straightforward: if you worked hard, you did well. It was my secret aim to earn the second- or third-highest grades in my class: that was where I would be happiest. And I was getting closer and closer as my English improved.

Often I made the long walk to school with a scrap of paper in one hand, reading a list of new words over and over again. In the other hand I carried my hard little school case, which grew heavier and heavier with each step. I wished I could carry my books in one of those backpacks that hung by straps from the shoulders. But only boys wore them, the popular boys slinging them casually over just one shoulder. When Mr. Kagan saw the calluses on my palm and fingers one night, he showed me how to tape a thick sponge around the handle of my case, and that made it a little more comfortable.

For one reason, I actually enjoyed the long walk to and from Caledon Street. On the way home I always rested for a while in my favorite place in Cape Town, which was called simply the Gardens. The Gardens was a park mainly composed of a gracious, long, wide pedestrian avenue through the heart of the city. Huge oak trees formed a cool arch above the avenue, and many people of different colors sat on the benches and chatted or dozed.

I loved the Gardens mainly because of the squirrels. The first morning that I walked along the avenue, I was startled to see a little creature peering at me from a grassy side path, balancing on its hind legs and wrinkling its nose in a thoughtful way over raised front paws.

I stopped and stared. The squirrel stared back. I blinked. The squirrel blinked, too. I laughed out loud. I was shocked to hear myself laughing. What if someone noticed me? I hurried off down the path toward school. When I dared to look back, only the squirrel was watching.

As soon as school ended that day, I hurried back to the Gardens, to the same spot, and sat down on a bench. Almost immediately, a squirrel scurried past and scrambled up a tree. Then another—a beautifully glossy squirrel—stopped to consider me, dug furiously for a few seconds, and carried the booty he had retrieved to a spot right under my bench, almost touching my legs. Delighted, I peered through the slats of the bench. He was eating a peanut in a wrinkled crunchy shell. I remembered seeing a vendor selling those peanuts in little paper cones at the entrance to the park. Were they meant for people or for squirrels? I wondered.

The next day I brought a few coins, knotted up in a corner of my handkerchief for safety, and timidly I purchased a cone of peanuts to feed the squirrels. It was the first time I had bought anything in my life, the first time I had had my own money. It came from the small allowance Mr. and Mrs. Kagan insisted on giving me each week.

"Got to have a few pennies," Mrs. Kagan had said genially.

"I don't need anything," I said awkwardly. It was embarrassing enough to take the clothes Mrs. Kagan bought for me. I reached out to return the money.

But Mr. Kagan pressed it gently back into my hand with his sweet smile.

"Thank you very much," I stammered.

Mrs. Kagan smiled proudly. "S'all right, dearie. Buy yourself some chocolates tomorrow, I'm sure, hey, dearie?"

But I kept every penny hidden in a box under my bed. What if things became bad again and there wasn't enough food? What if South Africans turned on the Jews as the Poles had done? What if I needed to get Naomi to a safe place?

The box was starting to feel wonderfully heavy. When I finally opened it to take out a few coins, I carefully subtracted the amount from the total I'd scribbled on a little piece of paper.

Today, in the Gardens, I had an offering for the squirrels, to thank them for the gift of their dark, steady eyes and the S-curve of their fat gray tails. And, I admit, to entice them closer.

One afternoon, as I was feeding the squirrels, a girl

walked past, then stopped and sat at the far end of the bench. When two squirrels bumped noses in their eagerness to reach a single peanut, I heard a soft laugh join my own giggle. I looked up. The girl was wearing the same school uniform that I wore and she seemed vaguely familiar, but I couldn't remember her name.

"Hello," she said shyly, pushing her short blond hair behind her ears.

"Hello," I answered. I couldn't think of anything else to say.

"You're one of those orphanage children from Europe," the girl stated.

She said it without unkindness, but I had to correct her. "I don't live at the orphanage. I live with the Kagans, in a flat."

"I live in a flat, too. We moved to Cape Town from Oudtshoorn last month," she offered, pushing her hair back again, although it was clearly too short to stay there. "My name's Monica Meisner."

"Mine's Devorah Lehrman."

Another awkward silence. We both turned to the squirrels.

"There are more squirrels than people here," I noticed suddenly, and we both started to laugh. Monica wasn't perfectly pretty, but when she laughed, her healthy white teeth showed and her brown eyes crinkled and her hair escaped, and she made me want to laugh, too.

"Maybe this is squirrel country and we are the ones

who are the visitors," Monica said.

"And maybe the squirrels should buy chocolate at the café and throw us tiny bits with their claws," I added.

"And we'd have to pick up the chocolate with our teeth!" Monica giggled. Then she stopped. "Hey, that makes me hungry. Let's walk to the bakery and I'll share a raisin bun with you."

My mouth watered. Mrs. Kagan sometimes bought those buns for tea. They had plump, squishy raisins inside and liquid sugar dribbled on the top. My hand went into my pocket to feel the precious pennies there. I probably had enough if we were going to share. "Let's go," I said.

By the time Monica and I parted, we had agreed to walk as far as the Gardens together the next day after school. And after that, it was simply understood that we would leave school together every day. The Gardens was our giant hideout, an enormous private club where we were the only human members, or at least the only ones we noticed.

"Other kids have a tree house; we have a whole park!" Monica said one day when we lay at the foot of our favorite old oak. As we gazed up into the different world of leaves and branches, my hair ribbon slipped off and I sat up and began capturing my long hair into a neat braid.

"Why do you always tie your hair back so tightly?" Monica asked. "If I had waves like yours instead of my thin straight hair, I'd show it off all the time. Here, have a look in my pocket mirror. See how pretty it is hanging loose. Especially with your dark eyes."

I peeked in the mirror. My cheeks were rosy and healthy and my eyes were framed by rich, flowing locks. Why had I never noticed before? Where was the strained, drawn face that used to look back at me? I grunted self-consciously and returned the mirror. The sun was warm on my back as I leaned comfortably on my elbows with my chin in my palms and looked down into the lawn. Between the green blades I could see cool, damp earth.

> "God, I can push the grass apart
> And lay my finger on Thy heart!"

"What are you mumbling?" Monica asked.

"Nothing really." I laughed. "It's just a poem by Edna St. Vincent Millay that I like. Hey, look at this beetle. I'm forcing him to turn left or right, but he's so cautious that he can't decide which way to go. So he's stuck!"

"I know someone as cautious as that," Monica said mischievously. "I've even seen her looking over her shoulder sometimes."

"I don't!" I protested.

"Oh, so you're admitting it's you," Monica teased. "Well, only occasionally. Like once an hour."

I had to laugh at the exaggeration. I still felt anxious at times, scared of a danger I couldn't predict. But with Monica I felt much safer. It wasn't simply that she, too, was Jewish. It was that Monica gave me the feeling she would help me out just as I would help her, if need be. Before, I'd been taking care of my sister. Now I had a friend.

Then came visits to Monica's flat. It was a home like no other I had ever been in, and I was a different person there, laughing and chatting easily in the friendly chaos. Monica's adored older brother, Max, and her easygoing parents, Mr. and Mrs. Meisner, lived in an extraordinarily untidy, noisy, and warm space, with a puppy, two parakeets in a cage, a goldfish tank, which was Max's pride, and a large cardboard carton holding Monica's two white mice and their nine offspring.

"Nine," Mr. Meisner had groaned when they dragged him over to see the tiny, bare morsels, blindly nudging at their mother. "Do you realize that means I'm supporting eighteen creatures in this household and that doesn't even include the goldfish? Eighteen! No wonder mouse fathers eat their babies!"

"They don't!" I protested.

"It happened when my friend Tony's mice had babies a few years ago," Max confirmed, and Monica turned to him. Monica trusted everything Max said.

"How can we stop the father from eating our babies?" she asked.

"I'll move the father to another box for a week or two," Max offered. He reached for a cardboard carton that was lying under a table and casually dumped out of it a pile of newspapers and a mess of coins, pencils, and keys. "Here, cut some newspaper into thin strips and we'll make another bed for him."

In a few minutes the papa had been separated from his new offspring, and the living room floor was covered with fine snippets of newspaper.

Monica stroked the father mouse crouching at the bottom of the big box. "He looks a bit lonely," she said doubtfully.

"Why don't we draw a few mice on the box walls for him to look at?" I suggested.

"Good idea," agreed Monica. "It's like hanging a mirror in a birdcage to keep the bird company."

Mrs. Meisner offered to find paintbrushes and a box of paints for "the young interior decorators."

"Daddy, you hold the father mouse while we paint," Monica demanded. Mr. Meisner took the creature gingerly.

"Man-to-man," Max joked.

"Can I try painting?" I asked. "I've never used a paint-brush before." There was a moment's silence as the Meisners looked at one another in apparent disbelief and then Monica passed over the brush quickly.

It wasn't like drawing with a finely sharpened pencil or even with a crayon; the first stroke didn't go at all where I expected. The brush was hairy and clumsy and it smeared color against the cardboard. I bit my lip in frustration. Then I dipped just the very tip of the brush in the paint again and tried making finer brushstrokes. That was better. Carefully, I brushed the outline of a round mama mouse standing in front of her babies, her claws raised to protect them from a tall, scary father mouse. I made the father's teeth disproportionately large and gave the plump mama an apron.

The Meisners' exclamations of praise made me blush. I suddenly remembered the man on the ship who'd told me I was talented.

"You're a very good artist," Max said.

I memorized his words. Later, when I was alone in my bedroom, I'd be able to mouth them, and maybe I'd even make up a scene in which he said what he'd said, and I would answer him very cleverly, but casually, of course, and then he would laugh as he bent over me, in order to look at the painting, of course, and I would smell his clean, boyish smell and admire his warm, lopsided smile from very close.

"Hey, dreamer," Mr. Meisner teased me. "Sign your initials in the corner and then go and wash that paint off your hands. It's nearly dark, so I'll drive you home."

# MRS. KAGAN IN CHARGE
## 1923

School was different now. Or maybe I was different. There was one girl I had always been careful to avoid. Her name was Heather Smith, and I was never sure why she made me uneasy; she just seemed surly. Then one day I nearly tripped over her when I was hurrying out to recess. She had bent down to tie her shoelace and I didn't see her and stumbled right into her back. "Sorry!" I said as I hopped clumsily to the side. She'd been knocked off her precarious balance, pitching forward onto her knees, not hard, but clearly enough to rouse a sudden fury.

"You'd better be very sorry, you bloody Jew," she said.

I took a step back immediately. Here it was, Poland again, pogrom again, fear again. But this wasn't Poland, it was my new place, and she was just Heather Smith, and suddenly I was angry. "What did you call me?" I asked in a voice that started off strangled and low.

"Bloody Jew. You're a bloody Jew," she repeated. And I

understood she had been wanting to say it for a long time.

"You say that again and I'll slap your face." The words just came out, and my fists went up in front of me.

"What's going on?" a familiar voice asked behind me.

"She called me a bloody Jew," I repeated to Monica as I glared at Heather.

In an instant Monica was squarely at my side. "Who do you think you are, Heather Smith?" she said. "You think you're better than we are?"

Heather seemed to size Monica up, then turned back to me. Her mouth was sneering, but there was a hint of uncertainty in her eyes. Her outburst had been interrupted and she'd lost a little steam, but she wasn't out of the ring yet.

"My dad says you're a bunch of dirty immigrants and our country shouldn't have to give you free education," she said.

I opened my mouth, but someone beat me to a reply. "Dirty immigrants?" a boy named Lenny Friedman shot back at her from just behind me. How had he come up so quickly? And he wasn't alone—he had three friends with him, Shlayma from the orphanage and two South African Jewish boys. "Take a look at your filthy fingernails, Heather. And how about washing your hair this month?"

One of the South African boys weighed in. "As for free education, you're going to be repeating this grade just like you repeated the last one, so don't talk to us about costing the government money."

I was buoyed, surrounded by support. Everyone wanted to say something, to shout after Heather as she slunk away. My strength was no longer needed. But I knew I had it.

One Saturday I returned home from an afternoon with Monica, feeling energy bubbling in me. I had cut my hair to shoulder length the previous week—just short enough that I didn't have to tie it back—and I shook it every now and again to feel the swish of freedom. Mr. and Mrs. Kagan listened as I told them about Monica's new puppy, Goldie.

"Goldie suddenly saw the neighbor's cat and he ran toward her. He was so excited to have a friend. And then she hissed, and she arched her back into the air, and all her hair stood on end. She must have almost doubled in size. Well, Goldie skidded to a halt. He fell over his big paws and he yelped. Then he turned around and came charging back to us as fast as he could. He was squealing like a pig! And he wouldn't climb out of Monica's arms until we were back inside their house."

Mrs. Kagan had been smiling at me while she knitted. "Our Devorah seems like a new child," she said to Mr. Kagan proudly.

The approval in her voice helped me muster the courage to make a request. "Would it be— May I— Monica says I can have one of her mice to take home if it's all right with you."

"Mice?" Mrs. Kagan repeated. Mr. Kagan blinked

nervously. It was not a good sign when Mrs. Kagan repeated something.

"It's just a little mouse. And very white and clean," I offered.

"Clean?" Mrs. Kagan did it again. I sent an imploring glance to Mr. Kagan, but he just looked at me sadly.

"I could keep it in a big box in my bedroom and I promise I'd take care of it myself," I tried desperately.

"Not in this flat, you won't. Mice belong in the fields. Can't think why you'd want one of those things," Mrs. Kagan said, and obviously that was that.

There was a quiet movement at the door and Elizabeth came in to take away the tea tray. Quickly I jumped up to help her so that Mrs. Kagan wouldn't see the tears welling in my eyes. Elizabeth clicked her tongue sympathetically, but after a quick glance at Mrs. Kagan, she said nothing.

Mrs. Kagan kept knitting, acting as if the mouse incident had never happened, so rather sulkily I said good night and walked out of the living room. But I purposely didn't close the door tightly and hovered in the hallway to hear if they would reopen the subject. Mrs. Kagan's needles clicked rapidly as she worked on a sweater for me.

"A new child, did I say?" Mrs. Kagan said. "Transformed, that's how our Devorah looks now. Thin little scrap she was when we brought her home. Less than two years ago. Her face so strained. And now? Filled out beautifully. Nothing like food and love to make a child fill out. And clever, too, how she studies. Never need to nag her to do her homework."

I heard a grunt of agreement from Mr. Kagan and that was all. He was probably drifting into a doze, head propped against the back of the hard sofa.

At least there was an unexpected little comfort in my room: a light, crumbly scone in a brown paper bag on my pillow. As soon as I smelled it, I knew who it was from. Once I had been sent with a message up to Elizabeth in the servants' quarters on the top floor of the building, and the aroma of sweet, dusty scones had filled the tiny room where Elizabeth was sitting with a friend.

As I nibbled at Elizabeth's gift, I remembered that that same day in her room, I had seen in a cheap frame a photograph of a solemn girl a few years older than I, with Elizabeth's high cheekbones. "How old were you when that photograph in your room was taken, Elizabeth?" I had asked the following day.

She looked confused for a moment, then said with a little laugh, "Aai, Miss Devorah, that is not me, that is my daughter. You think she looks so much like me? She's a good girl, that one."

Why hadn't I ever considered that Elizabeth might have her own family? I opened my mouth to ask her where her daughter lived and how she ever managed to see her, given that Elizabeth worked five or six long days a week in the flat and usually slept upstairs. I opened my mouth;

I closed it again. The question was too personal. But I thought sometimes about that girl, who saw her mother much less than I did.

The scone was nearly all gone and I wondered, as I often did, why Mrs. Kagan had ever adopted me. I had never dared to ask why she didn't have her own child. Perhaps Mr. Kagan's illness had something to do with it. Whatever the physical reason, I could picture Mrs. Kagan saying firmly to her husband, "Well, if we can't make a child, we'll just get one somewhere else, that's all," and marching him up the driveway to the Cape Jewish Orphanage.

I had to smile at the image. But then I remembered how cross I felt. How a little mouse, with its companionable squeaks and rustlings, would have kept me company in my room. And how unreasonable Mrs. Kagan was.

About two weeks later, after school, Mrs. Kagan interrupted my homework and insisted I join her for a drive. Within minutes I was clinging to the armrest on the car door as if it could save me when the crash came. I was quite sure that a crash was coming. Mrs. Kagan had a driver's license, but that didn't mean she could drive. She'd never had much practice because she and Mr. Kagan didn't own a car; they borrowed this old one from a friendly neighbor for special occasions.

What is the occasion today? I wondered for the tenth time. It was no use asking Mrs. Kagan again. She would just smile, place her forefinger hard against her own lips and then against my lips, and say, "Wait and see the surprise, dearie!"

It was best to concentrate on trying to stay in the slippery seat as the car hurtled around cliffs and bends, the ocean a sheer drop very close to our right side. White sand beaches gave way to ragged steps of massive boulders along the coast. Mrs. Kagan drove the way she lived: full speed ahead, obstacles notwithstanding. Leaning forward over the steering wheel, she powered the car with her own energy. The car roared and swung from side to side, but Mrs. Kagan held it together, and in the right direction, with her two strong hands.

We turned inland, leaving the ocean churning behind us. Quite soon we were making our way through the most beautiful farmland I had ever seen: white-plastered farmhouses with the lower lines of their roofs curved like a treble clef; soft green hills you could roll down and never bump yourself; sheep and plump cows and horses. Suddenly I remembered the horse Papa had had to sell and the way he had gone on pulling the heavy cart himself. Papa. Papa.

"We're here!" Mrs. Kagan declared gaily as she swung off the paved road and onto a gravel driveway, barely slowing down and narrowly missing a sign that said GROOTBOOM PLAAS. Freshly painted letters on a piece of cardboard hanging below spelled out: KATJIES TE KOOP.

*Grootboom Plaas* means "big tree farm" in Afrikaans. I

worked it out as we bounced to a halt in front of a barn. *Te koop* is "to sell," and *kat* is "cat." The *jies* at the end means "little," so *katjies* must mean "little . . ." I turned abruptly to stare at Mrs. Kagan. Could it be?

But my adoptive mother was already out of the car and bustling off to meet the farm woman who had emerged from the barn. *"Ek is Mevrou Kagan,"* she introduced herself in Afrikaans, shaking the woman's hand vigorously. "Called you last week. Glad we made it here. Good directions, you gave me. Let's see the kittens, then. Little girl's been longing for a pet."

Longing? I was lightheaded with joy.

"Come on, Devorah!" Mrs. Kagan shouted from inside the barn. I tumbled out of the car, sniffing at the scents of horses and hay and droppings I remembered from Domachevo. "Here's your surprise. Just take your pick."

The choosing was delicious. Under the suspicious gaze of the mother cat, I leaned into a straw-lined bin to count seven perfect kittens mewing and burrowing. I lifted the first soft body, slipping my fingers along the tiny bones and caressing the deep hollows between them. Would this be my own kitten, running to meet me when I returned from school? Would Mrs. Kagan let the kitten sleep on my bed, maybe?

*"Ja, nee,* yes, no. Take your time." The farm woman smiled. "I'll be in the house."

I picked up another kitten, nuzzled it, put it down gently next to its mother, changed my mind again and again.

Mrs. Kagan waited with surprising patience. Finally she set a limit. "Five more minutes, now. Have to get back in time for supper and Mr. Kagan waiting to see your happy face."

Five minutes! I moved back and forth between a tiny white kitten, as creamy as milk, and a playful ginger morsel with stripes like a miniature tiger. I lifted the white one again.

"This one," I said when Mrs. Kagan consulted her watch.

"That one?" Mrs. Kagan asked, eyeing the kitten doubtfully. "It's the smallest of the litter, Devorah."

"Yes," I said simply and tucked her under my chin.

A few moments later, the kitten had been paid for and we were back in the car and bumping down the driveway. I held the kitten on my lap, trying to keep her as calm as possible. But the kitten was uneasy. She clawed at my hands and even succeeded in scrambling up to my shoulder before I managed to grab her and pull her into my lap again. Big, frightened eyes darted from side to side.

I held her close with one hand and stroked gently with the other, but the cat mewed piteously, like a newborn baby. The cries went on and on, long minute after minute. "Why is she crying so much?" I asked.

"Misses the smell of her mother and sisters and brothers," Mrs. Kagan said matter-of-factly. "She'll get used to you."

With a frantic lunge, the kitten tried to escape from my grasp. I held on and must have squeezed too hard. The animal gave a yelp and then returned to her loud mewing.

"Please shh," I begged her.

"Just frightened," Mrs. Kagan observed.

Just frightened? I thought. Being frightened was such a terrible feeling that one couldn't place the word "just" in front of it.

"Stop the car," I said, my voice choking.

"What?" Mrs. Kagan asked, glancing at me in surprise.

"We have to get her back to her family," I started to say, and then, to my shame, I was crying. "I want to put her back with the others."

"You don't want her! After begging for a dirty mouse, and Mr. Kagan persuading me you really wanted a cat. And now this long drive. And the way you touched all those kittens. I could see you wanted one."

I was silent. The kitten kept mewing, butting and struggling against me with her head.

Mrs. Kagan tried a different tack. "If you give her back, she won't be able to stay with her mother, you know. Someone else will come and choose her."

I thought about that for a moment. I knew I couldn't help the kitten in the future, but I could give her a little more time with her family right now. "I want to take her back to the farm," I whispered, and Mrs. Kagan gave up. Swinging the car around, she drove back to Grootboom Plaas in uncharacteristic silence.

While the puzzled farm woman repaid the money to a grim Mrs. Kagan, I went into the barn alone. I replaced the kitten and stroked her for a few minutes. She stopped mewing immediately and pressed very close into her mother's flank. I could barely see through my tears. But I made sure I wiped my face and blew my nose before I walked back to the car. I didn't want to break down again in front of Mrs. Kagan.

It was going to be a long drive. My hands and lap felt empty. There were a few white hairs on my skirt. How much had happened in such a short time, I thought, remembering my excitement when I first read the farm sign. Clearing my throat, I turned to Mrs. Kagan. "I'm sorry," I said. "I'm sorry I caused you trouble. Thank you for getting me a kit—" I swallowed hard. "Thank you for offering me a kitten, anyway."

Mrs. Kagan's plump face softened immediately. "That's all right, dearie. Can't say I understand, but that's all right."

We drove through the dusk together.

# "It's My Home"
## 1924

Returning home from school one day, I was surprised to have the door opened rapidly not by Elizabeth but by Mr. Kagan. He was usually resting at this time, but today he was up and dressed and obviously excited.

"Devorah, my girl, at last. I have something to tell you. I had an interesting visit from Mr. Ochberg this morning."

Fear skipped in my stomach. Why would Daddy Ochberg visit in the morning? He knows I'm in school. Did the visit mean that Daddy Ochberg had arranged to move me away from the Kagans? Did I want that?

Mr. Kagan barely waited to close the door behind me. "He wants me to take a photograph of you. It has to be a very special photograph, because it's going to be . . ." He stopped for emphasis. "It's going to be in a book."

"Of me. A photograph. A book," I said, as though I didn't have a brain in my head.

"Someone is writing a book about the Jews of Poland. Before the Great War and after, the good times and the bad, the pogroms, everything. They want a picture of a young girl who survived. That's you."

I stared at Mr. Kagan. I had never heard him so talkative.

"There is someone writing down the stories?" I asked carefully.

"Yes, yes." He positively beamed. "Someone is going to write it all down so that people will remember. And you are going to be in it as a new start, a new life. And I am to be the photographer."

He was so proud, so glad. For the first time, I stepped forward and gave him a hug. He hugged me back and kissed my forehead. Then he hurried off to his darkroom. "To tidy up a little," he said.

Walking carefully, as though rough movements might break a dream, I entered my little room. I shut the door quietly and wedged my chair under the doorknob so no one could come in to interrupt me. Then I stood at the window and shut my eyes. There was no black sky with shining stars to talk to; I would have to imagine.

"Mama, Papa, wake up, I need to tell you something important. It's this: the stories won't be forgotten. Remember, Papa, when I promised at the cemetery? I promised I wouldn't let the stories be forgotten. It's been so hard, Papa, just as you warned me, and so lonely. But now there is help. There is to be a book, a book that will tell it all.

The good times and the bad, Mr. Kagan said. And can you believe it: my picture will be in the book, too. They say I am a new start. Mama, I am to be a new start."

Then I cried.

It was my photo that was to be used in the book, but stories had to be collected from several of the children who had begun their lives in Poland. Daddy Ochberg was very involved in the project and he drove me to the orphanage several times, where he gently but lengthily questioned the other children and me about details of our childhood. After one such session, as he drove me home, he asked me how it felt to be a Kagan now. The question touched a sore spot, a hurt I rubbed often to keep it from healing.

"I'm not a Kagan. They didn't care enough to change my name to Kagan. I'm Devorah K. Lehrman," I said sulkily.

Mr. Ochberg looked keenly at my face. "Legally speaking, that is true," he said. "The adoption papers say that you must retain your own name, in case there is ever an attempt by someone from your old life to trace you. So the Kagans were able to give you only a new middle name."

I frowned. "But Nechama became Naomi Stein."

"We cannot enforce what she is called every day," Mr. Ochberg said, shrugging. "But legally her last name is still Lehrman, just like yours. Now here we are at your home; I will see you next week."

As I stepped out of the car, tiny gears shifted inside my

head. Naomi and I still had the same name. And the Kagans were only following the law.

During the two years that passed after Naomi and I were adopted, I went several times a year to see her at the Steins' house. But there always seemed to be a reason why Naomi couldn't manage to come over to the Kagans' flat: a ballet recital, or a piano lesson, or a sudden cold. Finally, a date was set for Naomi to visit me.

When my sister first walked into the flat, I stared. Naomi looked like a Stein. Her clothes were expensive and much too smart for a casual visit. Her pretty light curls were tied with an enormous bow, and there was a mysterious pink shine to her lips, although she had only recently turned twelve. She was an exotic flower amid the dark furnishings of Caledon Street.

"Hello, Mrs. Kagan. Hello, Mr. Kagan," Naomi said formally. She was taking acting and elocution lessons, and her Yiddish accent had almost disappeared.

Mr. Kagan only smiled shyly, but Mrs. Kagan was determined to be warm. "Hello, Naomi. And how is your mother? Fine woman, and always so busy. See her hurrying all the time. So many committees, I know. Does such good work for charity. Well, isn't that a pretty—sit down here, Naomi?—pretty frock, can see that one wasn't made at home. Perhaps, Devorah, dearie, you might prefer—"

"Yes, we'll go into my room, if that's all right," I interjected, seeing Naomi's look of bewilderment, and we escaped from the living room together.

I took my sister into my bedroom and showed her a couple of books I was reading. The room felt cozy when Monica came over, but now it seemed too small for Naomi's full skirts.

"Where's that photograph you were always looking at?" Naomi asked, looking around.

I glanced at her for a moment, surprised that she remembered. Naomi evidently expected to see it displayed prominently, no doubt framed in silver like the ones of "family" members in her pink room. I opened a bottom drawer and pulled out the old photograph. It was dog-eared and a little faded. I hadn't noticed that. Actually, I realized, I hadn't taken it out for a while.

"Devorah, taking Mr. Kagan to his visit at the doctor. Prob'ly wait there till doctor's done with him," Mrs. Kagan said, putting her head in the doorway. "Elizabeth's put out sponge cake and juice for you two young ladies in the living room. So nice to have you at our home, Naomi. You quite ready, Mr. Kagan?" And she was gone.

With the bang of the front door, Naomi seemed bolder. "Let's go to the living room," she said brightly. "There's no space here."

I put the photograph back in the drawer and followed her. Elizabeth came in to check if we needed anything, and I felt proud to show off my sister's finery. But Elizabeth didn't show any sign of being impressed. I did notice that Naomi didn't bother to thank Elizabeth for pouring juice, as Mrs. Kagan had taught me to do.

We began playing a board game Monica had lent me, but Naomi was more interested in talking. "Daddy's going to buy a bioscope," she announced. "He said as soon as he's the owner, I can go to the moving pictures whenever I want. I'll ask him to give you a ticket."

My emotions warred. A free ticket to the pictures. But the way Naomi said "daddy" so easily made my eyelid twitch.

Then Naomi jumped to another thought, as was her way. "Has anyone else from the orphanage been adopted?" she asked.

"I don't think so," I replied. "Faygele told me once that she doesn't want to be adopted, that she doesn't need new parents and she likes being there."

"Well, she doesn't know what she's talking about," Naomi said smugly. "We're the lucky ones."

That took me aback. Naomi was including me among the lucky ones. And Mr. Bobrow had called me lucky when Daddy Ochberg asked to interview me in Pinsk. Madame Engel, too, had said something about the lucky few. Yet I had never thought of myself that way.

Right then, Naomi looked at her pretty silver wrist-watch for the third time. "I think we should go and get my things from your room," she said. "Then I'll be ready when I have to go."

While Naomi sat on the bed folding her white cardigan and checking her little coin purse, I heard the front door bang shut. I wondered why Elizabeth hadn't come to say goodbye before she left. It was her weekend off and I wouldn't be seeing her again until Monday morning. Quickly I moved toward my open door to shout out goodbye. But at the exact same moment, Naomi stood up and stepped forward. We were so close that we bumped hard into each other. With a little cry, Naomi fell back onto the bed.

"Oh, sorry!" I exclaimed, although it wasn't my fault.

"This room is too small," Naomi snapped, smoothing down her skirt. "I don't know how you can sleep here and do your homework and everything. Why, the cupboard for my mother's clothes is bigger than this."

I glared at her. How could she be so rude? But I didn't want our visit to end badly.

"Let's go back to the living room, then," I said shortly.

"No, I don't want to wait there, either," Naomi shot back. "All those photographs staring down at us are creepy."

"Mr. Kagan's a very good photographer," I began, my loyalty to kind Mr. Kagan aroused.

But Naomi wasn't to be stopped. "And the furniture's so uncomfortable and old-fashioned," she said, her voice rising shrilly. "And what are those silly lace doilies doing on the arms and backs of the chairs? They're meant to go on a cake plate underneath a cake. I know because I've seen our cook use them."

"Your cook!" I retorted, also becoming louder. "Why

do you think she knows better than Mrs. Kagan does?"

"Mother says Mrs. Kagan doesn't have any taste. And that she never stops talking—and that's true."

For a moment I couldn't breathe. My heart pounded loudly, once, twice, like a drum echoing in my chest. "You shut your mouth, Nechama Lehrman," I exploded. "Have you forgotten where you come from? You've got cheek to criticize the Kagans. They're good people. They're good to me. They've got rich hearts."

Naomi shrank back against the bed, looking frightened. But I wasn't finished. "You hold your nose so high in the air that you can't see what's in front of you. This flat may not look like a lot to you, but it's my home and I'm safe and I feel good here. I have a family now, too."

Naomi was speechless. I listened to my own words ringing in the air. When had my feelings changed, without my even noticing? A sudden lightness filled me like helium. I was at home.

I took a long, slow look around. My precious books. The desk where I spent so many hours. The roses I had air-dried carefully after Mr. Kagan brought them home for me one Shabbes. The calendar of a girl and a kitten, which Mrs. Kagan had given me with a hug soon after our drive to Grootboom Plaas. And there, looking miserable as she pressed against the bed with her fancy dress crumpled beneath her, was my little sister.

Impulsively, I said, "It's all right, Naomi. I know you didn't mean to be rude. I don't expect you to understand.

But it's finally turned out that you're happy and I'm happy. That would make Mama and Papa happy."

Naomi's lip quivered as if she was going to cry. But I had learned enough not to make the same mistake again, not to assume the old role of the comforting big sister. Instead I held out my hand, simply. And, simply, Naomi took it and squeezed.

At that moment, there was the rude *baarp baarp* of a car honking outside. "That's Daddy's driver from work," Naomi exclaimed with unhidden relief. She dropped the little coin purse into her black patent handbag, and I went outside with her. Before Naomi climbed into the back of the large car, we turned to each other awkwardly, and then we hugged tightly.

The car pulled away and there was only stillness. The sun was blindingly hot, the air white. I walked slowly back into the flat and stopped just inside the front door. The cool dimness welcomed me. I inhaled the faint scents of furniture polish and photo-developing chemicals and sponge cake. I like the smells here, I realized.

Smiling, I turned toward my room, and then I heard something—muffled, faint sobs. They were coming from the Kagans' closed bedroom.

In the space of a heartbeat, I understood what had happened. The door that banged before was Mrs. Kagan arriving home early. She must have heard Naomi's loud, cruel words. Her carefully arranged framed photographs, the living room furniture polished to a high shine, the space under the stairs turned into a bedroom for me with energy and care—all ridiculed and insulted by a little rich girl who didn't know that love came in plain as well as fancy packages.

I ran down the hallway, pulled open the bedroom door, and flung my arms around the woman sobbing on the bed. "I'm so sorry!" I cried. "Please don't be sad. She doesn't know anything about our family. I'm so sorry."

In an instant Mrs. Kagan had turned and encircled me with her own strong arms. We hugged and cried together. Then Mrs. Kagan walked over to get a handkerchief and blew her nose thoroughly. Sitting down on the bed again, she took my hand in hers. "Those were happy tears, dearie," she said. She spoke in careful, full sentences as if every word was vital. "This is one of the happiest days of my life."

"It is?" I asked, bewildered. "Didn't she hurt your feelings?"

"Yes, she did," replied Mrs. Kagan slowly. She reached out a trembling hand to smooth one of the offending lace doilies on the glass side table. "I didn't grow up with money, and when I can afford it, I buy things I think are beautiful. I didn't know some people think my taste is low class. But that's not important."

"It isn't?"

"No, it isn't," Mrs. Kagan said, giving my hand a squeeze as she looked directly into my eyes. "What is important is that today I heard my daughter saying that she is happy in her life, saying that she is comfortable in her home, even saying that she feels good here. Family, you called us. When I heard that, my heart filled with joy. Nothing else matters."

I looked back at her, and for a moment I heard Madame Engel saying, "Hold on to the strength . . . let go of the sadness." Tears were rolling down my cheeks and I didn't mind at all anymore that Mrs. Kagan saw them. It was the right time to say something. I hadn't told Mama and Papa yet, but I would explain it to them at the window after my evening prayers.

"I— Is it all right if—?" I started. "I would like—"

Mrs. Kagan's face was quite old, rather wrinkled, and very kind. "What is it, dearie?"

"I would like—" I stopped and smiled. "I'd like to call you Mummy."

# AFTERWORD

In her early twenties, Devorah Lehrman married Chaim Wulf, and they soon had a son and a daughter. Sixteen years later, they had a third child (now the author's husband), who grew up and went to medical school at the University of Cape Town. When, three years in a row, he won an academic award funded by the Ochberg Foundation, he tried to thank the foundation staff for their thoroughness in continuing to assist the descendants of the original orphans. But he found that they had no role in selecting the award winners. Isaac Ochberg had touched two generations of the same family by coincidence.

Other coincidences lit the long path in the evolution of this book. Devorah's first son married the daughter of Ochberg orphan Rosha, and Devorah's second grandson married the granddaughter of Ochberg orphan Laya, although there were only 200 Ochberg children in the large South African community of over 100,000 Jews. The author's maternal great-aunt, Rebecca Levinson, was the matron, or house mother, of the Cape Jewish Orphanage in Cape Town only a few years before the children arrived from Europe. The author's paternal aunt, Rhoda Stella Getz, was a volunteer librarian at the orphanage after the Ochberg children grew up.

When they were in their sixties, first Naomi and then Devorah died of breast cancer. Although they saw each other fairly regularly throughout their lives, the sisters' relationship had been forever changed by their separation and different fortunes.

Isaac Ochberg served as president of the orphanage for several more years, but in 1930 he gave up his work with the children, partly for health reasons and partly to work for the development of what was then Palestine (Israel). He died of stomach cancer at age fifty-nine, a year before World War II began. For many years, on the anniversary of his death, the Ochberg children recited the Mourners' Kaddish, a prayer said only by close relatives of the deceased, as if Isaac Ochberg had been their father. Alexander Bobrow married, moved to England, and lived into his nineties. Lively little Faygele Shrier became Mrs. Fanny Lockitch and had three sons, but stayed involved with the orphanage, serving as chairwoman for five years. She was of invaluable assistance in the writing of this book. In 1991, the few children still living in the Cape Jewish Orphanage (usually known as Oranjia) were moved to small group homes, and the building was sold and demolished.

## Author's Note

From the end of the eighteenth century, the Polish people in Eastern Europe were dominated by the Russian empire, under the Czar. While Russia was engaged in the Great War (now called World War I) with the Germans from 1916 to 1918, revolution broke out inside Russia and the Czar was overthrown. The revolutionaries also fought among themselves, the "Reds" (Communists) battling the "Whites" (anti-Communists). The Poles entered the chaos in a fight for their longed-for independence.

Domachevo [Doh-ma-CHAIR-wah], the village where this story is partly set, lay close to the fluctuating border between Poland and Russia, roughly equidistant from the main city of Warsaw and the town of Pinsk. Bands of soldiers from several armies—Polish, Red Russian, White Rus-sian, and German—passed through Domachevo. About thirty miles north was situated the town of Brest Litovsk, where the famous treaty that ended the war between Russia and Germany was signed in 1918.

During the time covered by the story, over two million Jews lived in Polish areas, about 10 percent of the population. Because they were forbidden to be farmers, professionals (such as doctors and lawyers), or craftspeople in almost any field, many Jews became shopkeepers and moneylenders, two of the few professions allowed them. This led to tensions when poor non-Jews borrowed money and could not pay it back. Rumors of hidden Jewish wealth were widespread, and hatred of Jews was fanned by many priests who claimed that the Jews had killed Jesus and were the root of all evil. Periodically, usually under the influence of liquor and sometimes led by Russian soldiers on horseback called Cossacks, local townspeople would erupt into sudden attacks, or "pogroms," in the Jewish part of town, burning, beating, and killing Jews.

One such attack inspired this work of historical fiction, based on what is known of the childhood of my late mother-in-law and her sister, and of the momentous rescue of the "Ochberg orphans." Isaac Ochberg, Alexander Bobrow, Regina Engel, Judge Joseph Herbstein, the Steins, the Kagans, Mr. Mark Cohen, Miss Rosa van Gelderen, and little Faygele (Fanny Shrier Lockitch) were real people who played important roles in the lives of Devorah [Duh-VOR-ah] and Nechama [nuh-KHA-mah] Lehrman, but I have fictionalized most of their actions and words. To the orphans in the book I have given the first names of children who were part of the actual group, in tribute, although no resemblance is intended.

—L.P.W.

# Glossary of Hebrew and Yiddish Words

Cholent (CHOH-luhnt)—A slow-cooking stew of beans, potatoes, and sometimes meat, traditionally prepared before the Sabbath and kept warm to be eaten at lunch on Saturday.

Kreplach (KREP-lekh)—Small dumplings filled with meat, cheese, or potato.

Mamaleh (MAH-muh-luh)—Literally, "sweet little mother," but often used to mean "sweet little girl."

Shabbes (SHAH-biss)—The day of Sabbath, which stretches from dusk on Friday to after nightfall on Saturday.

Shema (Shuh-MAH)—The central prayer of the Jewish religion, proclaiming the oneness of God, which is recited morning and evening.

Shiva (SHIH-vuh)—The traditional week of mourning after a Jew is buried, during which bereaved family members sit on cushions or a low couch, attended by visitors.

Shochet (SHOW-khet)—A slaughterer who is qualified by Jewish law to check that an animal is fit for consumption and to kill it in the quickest way.

Shtetl (SHTEH-t'l)—A small town or village where mostly Jews lived in Eastern Europe, up until the Second World War.

Shul (SHOOL)—Synagogue; a Jewish place of worship and study and also the center of the community.

Tsigele (TSIH-guh-luh)—A little goat.

Yarmulke (YAHR-muhl-kuh)—Skullcap or kippah, worn by most observant males at all times and by other Jewish males (and sometimes females) in the synagogue and while praying.